STORIES TO KEEP YOU ALIVE

DESPITE VAMPIRES

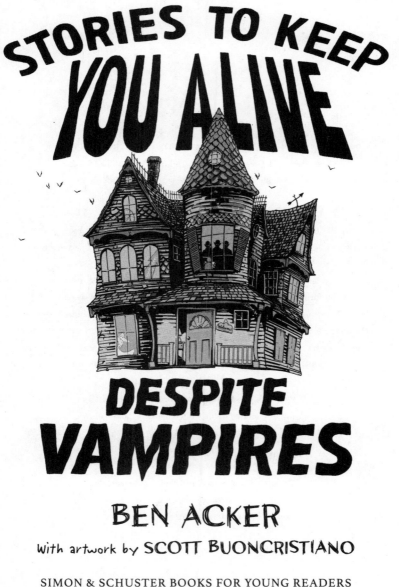

BEN ACKER

With artwork by SCOTT BUONCRISTIANO

SIMON & SCHUSTER BOOKS FOR YOUNG READERS

New York   London   Toronto   Sydney   New Delhi

SIMON & SCHUSTER BOOKS FOR YOUNG READERS

An imprint of Simon & Schuster Children's Publishing Division

1230 Avenue of the Americas, New York, New York 10020

Text © 2022 by Ben Acker

Illustrations © 2022 by Scott Buoncristiano

Book design by Laura Eckes © 2022 by Simon & Schuster, Inc.

SIMON & SCHUSTER BOOKS FOR YOUNG READERS

and related marks are trademarks of Simon & Schuster, Inc.

For information about special discounts for bulk purchases, please contact

Simon & Schuster Special Sales at 1-866-506-1949 or business@simonandschuster.com.

The Simon & Schuster Speakers Bureau can bring authors to your live event. For more

information or to book an event, contact the Simon & Schuster Speakers Bureau at

1-866-248-3049 or visit our website at www.simonspeakers.com.

The text for this book was set in Athelas.

The illustrations for this book were rendered digitally.

Manufactured in the United States of America

0722 FFG

First Edition

2 4 6 8 10 9 7 5 3 1

Library of Congress Control Number: 2022930989

ISBN 9781665917001

ISBN 9781665917025 (ebook)

To Neil Mahoney.
I wish this weren't the first
ghost story in this book.

DON'T READ THIS.

Obviously, *do* read this, just not out loud.

Read it to yourself as fast as you can. You never know when they'll come back, and you need to catch up quick if you're going to survive.

This book—this one you're holding in your hands—may be the only thing that stands between your survival and your total utter complete lack of survival.

Or . . .

(and *this* is the bad part)

. . . worse.

And no offense if *worse* happens to you, but if it does, it's because you didn't read this part fast enough, so please—I'm yelling now—*read faster!*

Obviously, if you've found this book where I left it, you're in that house on the corner that shouldn't be so dark but is so dark. Even during the brightest, bluest afternoon, daylight does not touch this house. The house stands in a shadow as dark as midnight! It may, in fact, be cast in midnight itself. Impossible? Yes! And yet, if you are reading this, you know it is also true.

And that is just the beginning of the impossible things about this house that are also true.

But enough talking about impossible things about this house that are also true; *there's no time!*

Did you walk too close to the gate? I walked too close to the gate. Then, I found myself inside the dark house on the corner. I found myself in the little—I don't know what you call it, the spot inside the door with the narrow, tall table where you put the mail. Not quite a room. There must be a name for it. There's a name for everything.

Someone once said, "There's power in names," but I can't remember who.

If I knew the name of that house-starting door-nook space, maybe I would have been able to say "What am I doing in this area that I know the name of? I do not belong here." Maybe that would have broken my trance and gotten me out the door, past that gate, and far away. Maybe I wouldn't be trapped in the house where it's always night.

Trapped by the creatures who occupy the night house. These creatures, these terrible, terrifying things stinking of death and hunger and, as touched on before, *worse*.

Entryway!

It's called an entryway, that mail-hall. That seems too simple, but some things are too simple. An entryway. What else is it, after all? And so, what else would you call it?

"Foyer," it occurs to me now that it is also sometimes called.

And what else would you call it but the house's undertow that brought me from the shore of the entryway out into the cold depths of the house to a room so far out that it felt useless to try to swim back in again?

Well, let this book, handwritten and hidden, wedged in between the impressive, intricately carved, antique mahogany bed frame and the inexpensive, poorly assembled, mostly particleboard nightstand, be your life jacket as you bob in place among conflicting design choices. Good for you for using crucial time to search your surroundings! You have found, I'm glad to tell you, just the book to help you through your stay in the—let us call it "guest room" where you are being kept.

Only you are no guest and it is no room!

You are, as I was, a captive.

And the guest room is, to continue the more poetic description of our surroundings, the middle of the ocean!

What did I say the book was? A life jacket? It's better than that, as proof against the sharks that inhabit these waters! It is a small wooden boat and a strong pair of oars that will, if piloted correctly, keep you from being savaged by the sharks below that represent the vampires within.

That's right: the sharks here are vampires! Merciless, puncture-toothed, nocturnal creatures who will poke holes in you and use those holes to drink you up.

But that's less important than the crucial part.

But what is the crucial part? Great question.

This is the crucial part—if you read nothing else, read this. Skip right to—if you're stuck back in the beginning few pages, skip right exactly to here—VAMPIRES ARE RULES-FOLLOWERS!

Vampires cannot enter your house without spoken permission

by a resident or occupant. Everyone knows this.

If a vampire—fewer people know this—if a vampire, once invited, chooses to enter, they must wipe their shoes clean or else take them off and roam about in sock feet. Warning: never try on a vampire's shoes. Living feet in the shoes of the undead do not tend to stay that way.

Vampires—nobody knows that this is an actual rule—are only permitted to drink people by the neck. "Other places might be redder, but necks are better," vampire rules say.

Vampires cannot stand garlic; it tastes like soap to them.

And if vampires—this is the crucial rule; please skip right to this one—if vampires have you in their house because their house is impossible but also true, the vampires cannot so much as nibble you if you tell them a story. If the story is any good at all, they may not cause you any harm. They must, in fact, keep you from harm to the best of their ability. This includes your care and feeding.

And so, I have provided for you in this volume the stories I invented for fear of death or worse during my period of captivity. I leave them here for you in case you cannot think up stories on your own.

Vampires prefer scary stories. They like them because there is a chance vampires will play a role in them.

If the vampires complain that they have heard these stories before, let them know that they are free to let you go at any time. Maybe that will work.

Good luck, my friend, which I call you even though I do not know you, for we have our capture in common. I hope I help you get out of this.

And now I present:

STORIES TO KEEP YOU ALIVE DESPITE VAMPIRES!

THE PHANTOM
OF THE HITCHHIKER:

The Hitchhiker Who Was the
Phantom of a Hitchhiker

There was a guy driving around, right? Nothing strange about that. In fact, it was pretty fun and great for the guy. He was sixteen years old, this guy, and driving a car was a whole new way for him to be in the world. He had just gotten his driver's license, and he was driving around, as I said.

Now, he had a coat on, this guy, because of how it was autumn. Even though he was in his car and it wasn't even that super cold out, just crisp.

Oh, I should also mention that it was night out. So. Very. Night.

The guy didn't care how night it was, though. His car had headlights!

Suddenly, around a quarter of the way through this story, the guy's car's headlights shone on a person. A girl around the same age as the guy stood by the side of Foxhound Road with her thumb out.

She was *hitchhiking*.

The guy decided to pick her up. He pulled over, popped the locks open, smiled, and gave her a friendly "come on in" wave. The hitchhiker put her thumb back to its normal position and slipped into the car as quiet as a hundred librarians.

"Where are you headed?" the guy asked. "My name's RJ," he said in a voice that felt about three years older than he was. The guy thought nineteen-year-olds had it all figured out.

Rather than answer the guy with words, like you're supposed to, because of manners, this hitchhiker just pointed.

Spooky, right? A little.

The guy would drive, and the hitchhiker would point, and the guy would drive where she pointed. A few times, the guy would try to talk to her. He liked to think, as some do, that the driver is the host of the car.

"Nice night," he'd say. She didn't say anything back or even nod.

"You go to school around here?" he asked, wondering if she went to any of the nearby schools and also wondering why she wasn't even nodding or shaking her head, if talking wasn't her thing.

It was getting spookier because while she wasn't shaking her head, the guy in this story, I think his name is RJ, noticed she was shivering.

He's nice. He offered her his coat, which she took without ever taking her eyes off the road ahead. He offered to turn on the heater, but she was back to guiding him using only her pointing pointer finger.

Down this road. Up another. Turn right. That sort of thing. You know how driving works. So they got to a cul-de-sac. The hitchhiker pointed one final point, to the top of a long driveway. She closed her fist as if to say "stop" and he stopped. She got out, quieter than when she got in.

Now, this driveway? It's a little totally spooky. There's, like, mist or something, but not only that.

Foreshadowing of some sort happens here. You just know the guy's gonna come back tomorrow to get his coat (that he is forgetting to get back just now), and he's going to find out something strange about this hitchhiker who, as far as he knows at this point, is not a phantom at all, so much as, he thinks, she is an alive person.

It's late. The guy drives home. On his way, he remembers about his coat. He even says out loud, "Oh! My coat!" He decides he'll get it the next day because he's closer to home than the cul-de-sac.

So. Next day. Two-thirds of the way through the story. The guy parks at the top of that long driveway. He gets out and there's that feeling of foreshadowing again. No mist, though. You just feel a little spooked. More you than the guy, even. You're ahead of him. That's a big part of it.

So the guy walks down this steep driveway, where he finds a house. The guy rings the doorbell. Some lady answers. A lady older than the guy, like, maybe forty or so? *A mom's age,* the guy thinks, and he's about to find out that he's right.

The guy explains his situation. That he dropped off a teenage hitchhiker there at the house last night. The guy gets no response from the lady.

The guy describes the hitchhiker. "She was kind of odd, didn't really talk. Dark blond hair."

Still the lady doesn't say anything.

The guy goes into even more detail: she had a thing about pointing, she liked to point. She had blue eyes.

And now the lady freaks out a little. "It sounds like you're describing my daughter, Meg," she says. "But it can't be her."

Now the guy starts to freak out. "Why not?"

Are you ready for this? The guy isn't.

"She *died* three years ago last night. In a terrible hitchhiking accident on Foxhound Road."

Which, if you remember, that's the name of the actual

road where the guy picked the hitchhiker up the night before.

"Whoaaa," the guy says. "That means that the hitchhiker I picked up was her ghost. Or phantom."

"Obviously," says the lady. "That is the most logical conclusion you could draw."

The guy leaves, because he doesn't know what else to do besides be completely freaked out from having driven a ghost or phantom around in his very own car. He leaves all like, "Whoa."

The lady watches him go. When the guy was good and gone, the lady closes the door, and she and her daughter—who was totally alive—giggle and high-five. They put that guy's coat on the pile with the others.

The others?

Yeah. The others.

Three years later, they would open a used-coat store.

And they would get rich off it. Just so rich.

DIAGNOSIS: WOLF

Ava went to visit her doctor.

"What seems to be troubling you, young lady?" asked Dr. Grish.

"I got bit by this creature." Ava sighed. She was twelve, and preferred not to be called "young lady." She showed him a fading bite mark on her arm. "It was like a wolf, but it walked standing up on two legs."

"Mm." The doctor nodded. "Happens."

"And ever since then, on every full moon, I get this sensation like I'm ripping out of my skin, and then it all goes dark. I wake up, mostly in fields. Often I'm covered in blood. Once I was lying on the dead body of a deer."

"Well, that all seems like it would be pretty disturbing."

"Good," said Ava. "That means I'm telling it right."

Dr. Grish sat and thought. He crossed his legs very tightly.

"My—" Ava started to say something else, but the doctor held up a "wait a sec" finger.

Dr. Grish tapped on his lips while puffing up his cheeks. He exhaled. He shook his head and clucked his tongue, then clicked his teeth. He made a real show of thinking for a good two minutes. It ended with a whistle that said he was all out of ideas.

"Gee, I just don't know. Maybe you're getting some details wrong. He looked her up and down. "It's usually diet. Could be allergies or puberty or a combination." He poked at his temple playfully with a pencil. "Anyway, I'd like to run a few tests."

He took out plastic medical containers of various sizes.

"Hang on," said Ava, confused. "You're about to do tests on me in case I'm wrong about what I said?"

"Exactly. Let's find out what it probably is instead of what you think."

"That's the thing," explained Ava. "I started to say. I know what it is. My mom told me."

"Is she a doctor?" the doctor asked.

Ava explained that her mother saw Ava turn into a

giant creature, like a wolf but, like the thing that bit her, this one—the one that Ava turned into—walked standing up.

The doctor made thinking sounds again with his tongue and teeth.

"No," he shook his head.

"'No'?" asked Ava. "'No' what? What 'no'?"

"Not 'no,'" said the doctor. "Not definitively 'no.' Just most probably not. Most definitely not, if I'm honest. Like 'for now' no. 'Pending tests I'm not prepared to run' no."

"She took pictures," Ava said. She showed Dr. Grish the series of pictures that captured her transformation into a great hairy beast.

"Inconclusive." He shook his head.

"This is the conclusion." Ava held up the last picture, where she was a giant lupine creature. "I just don't want to hurt anyone. I don't want to do to someone else what was done to me. I don't want to be this—wolf thing."

"Which is it?" asked Dr. Grish. "You just listed three things you don't want. Your story keeps changing. How am I supposed to make heads or tails of any of it?"

"Wait," said Ava. "When I said I was bit by a standing-up wolf, you said that happens. When does that happen? To whom?"

"Now, Eva—"

"Ava," Ava interrupted.

"Young lady, I cannot discuss the diagnoses of some patients with others."

"Some? Some of your patients have this? Then why couldn't I have it?"

"Ho ho, okay." Dr. Grish shook his head. "You? A young lady? A wolf*man*? Now I've heard everything."

"But why not?" she asked.

"The wolf*man* condition only affects *men*. Women, and girls especially, are too . . ."

Dr. Grish flapped his hands open and shut near his eyes and made high-pitched squeaks.

"But—" Ava started.

"It just wouldn't take," the doctor concluded.

"Is there a treatment for it, if it would?" she asked, watching the sun set outside.

"It wouldn't. But yes. There's a treatment I give to the men that get it. Couldn't be easier. It's a vitamin, really. You take it right before the full moon. Not you, you understand. Men."

"Could I try it just once and see?" she asked.

"That wouldn't be ethical, would it?" he asked, the moon rising behind him.

"Trust me," she said, "it would be worth it."

"Sorry, but trusting patients isn't what they teach you at doctor school," Dr. Grish said. "Hmm. Look at that.

Moon's up already. Full moon, too. Now, let's have you take these tests, and if you're really sweet, I'll give you a lollipop after. Would you like that, young lady?"

They were his very last words.

THICKER THAN WATER

The campfire crackled.

The campers itched and squirmed in their seats, waiting for the story to start. It's always so itchy to wait. The itchiest is waiting for a story to start.

"Do you know about Camp Pemdas?" Sevan stopped their itching by starting the story. "It was the math camp across the lake. It was basically school in the summer, outside and with cabins. They didn't have sports; they didn't have ping-pong. They had geometry. They had algebra. They had a waterfront, but they didn't have waterfront activities. Not like we do here. They used the lake to calculate area, circumference, and volume.

"That's where their troubles began. On the shore of Lake Tarleton. Rather than swimming, kayaking, and canoeing in its majestic waters, they did math instead." The campers kind of shuddered in not quite fear. They would not have liked to spend their summer graphing graphs or learning what cosecants are, but the story so far was not the kind of spooky a campfire promises. No monsters, ghosts, or killers. Not yet.

"Do you know about the Lurk of the Lake?" Sevan asked, introducing the story's monster. Some of the older kids nodded. Some of the younger kids shook their heads no. The rest of the kids didn't do anything noteworthy in terms of reacting. Not on the surface anyway. They were all more alert. A monster had been named. That sharpens the senses. It gives a feeling to the air. A vulnerable feeling. A feeling of being watched.

"The Lurk of the Lake is the amphibious terror lurking in the depths of the lake," Sevan continued. "Sharp and slimy and meaner than a snapping turtle with a toothache. He's a green that's as dark as shadow, a creature of magic and nature and the night. He is why we must all respect the lake. The Lurk is the lake's inky wrath. He is the lake's terrible punishment. He is the lake's final revenge."

"Revenge for what?" a young camper asked.

"Well," Sevan welled. "For example, if you went to

a camp on the lake and did math instead of waterfront activities."

The young camper gasped, as she had just heard an example of a whole camp dedicated to exactly that.

"One full moon, the Lurk of the Lake lurked to and from the lake, dragging Camp Pemdas campers two at a time from their bunks and into the water. Forever.

"There were a total of one hundred and fifty campers and thirty counselors. Every cabin held ten campers and two counselors. The cabin closest to the lake took the Lurk four minutes to get to from the lake and six minutes to return to the lake, longer because he was dragging campers or counselors. The cabin farthest from the lake took the Lurk six minutes to get to from the lake and eight minutes to return to the lake. While Camp Pemdas was the kind of camp that would figure out how long it took for the Lurk of the Lake to drag everyone into the lake and how many cabins there were, we are not that kind of camp. We at Camp Moosejaw are the kind of camp where we respect the lake." Sevan turned in the direction of the lake and gave a little salute.

"Don't disrespect the lake," she continued. "Do not disrespect it anywhere in the Lurk of the Lake's domain, which extends around the lake, past the camp, through the woods, up to the road to town." The campers took note of the Lurk's domain.

"Listen," whispered Sevan, as the sounds of the forest—the wind in the trees, the owl, the chorus of crickets and frogs—grew and grew.

"That's him. That's all him. The Lurk. He can hear everything. And everything you can hear, he can touch," Sevan said. "Take it from me. I'm in charge of waterfront activities. Don't disrespect the lake. That includes hanging up your life jackets when you're done using them. Or the Lurk of the Lake will eat you up."

The campers headed back to their cabins. Jin thought that the Lurk of the Lake was nonsense. Todd disagreed. He had heard from his older brother's best friend that there actually had been a massacre across the lake at the math camp last summer. Diya was on the fence. Then she was off the fence. She was a believer. It was as if she were looking right at it, because she was—in front of them.

The Lurk blended into the shadows of the forest. His bulbous black eyes shined in the darkness. The campers could make out some of this monster's features—sharp teeth, bony fingers. He smelled of duckweed and danger. His voice came from all around them.

"That campfire sssstory," hissed the Lurk. "Ssssome of it wasss true. I can hear all that goesss on in my foresst. Passst the road, though. Halfway to town, in fact. Counssselor got her factsss wrong there. Do not disssresssspect the lake. Thisss much isss true."

22

"Did you come to us to correct the record?" Todd, the least afraid boy, asked.

"Of courssse I did!" The trees groaned in borrowed anger. "But not about that. The math campersss were—in their way—very ressspectful of my lake."

"Then why did you kill them?" asked Jin, the most afraid boy.

"And how long did it take?" asked Diya, who liked word problems.

"I didn't kill them," the Lurk snapped, then took a breath to calm himself down. "That'sss what I want to tell you. Have you heard of Tarleton Jack?"

The creature told a story of a group of counselors from Pemdas who went to town on their day off some summers ago and made some bad judgments, errors, and miscalculations. The driver should not have been driving, and the passengers shouldn't have been in the car with that driver. They came around a harsh curve on the road and hit a man with the car. They panicked and threw his body into Lake Tarleton. They swore to each other to never tell anyone what they'd done.

"But I knew," the Lurk hissed. "And he knew. They killed him. Only, he wasssn't dead, sssso he plotted hisss ssssweet revenge. The next year, he, Tarleton Jack, terror-issssed thessse counsssselorsss. In return for killing him that day, a year ago, he killed them one by one.

"The lassst one begged, pleaded desssperately for her life. And then in the doing, realissssed sssomething. Tarleton Jack wasss alive. The counssselorsss hadn't actually killed him at all. They had at worssst merely inconvenienssssed him. He wasss vassstly overreacting. He wassss exsssacting revenge all wrong. He was taking revenge on people who didn't kill him.

"The counsssselor hoped Jack would let her go. Inssstead she made him realisssse how much more revenge he could take, by this new exsssspanded definition."

"So you're saying," said Diya, "that he killed everyone in an entire camp as revenge for them *not having* killed him?"

"Yesss."

"Come on." Todd shook his head.

"You don't believe me?" The Lurk held out his clawed webbed hands. "Why would I lie?"

"You are a monster," Todd pointed out. Diya and Jin agreed by nodding.

"Not that kind," the Lurk told them.

"Why are you talking to us instead of to Sevan?" Diya asked. "Sevan's the one telling wrong stories about you."

"Oh, I already sssspoke with Ssssevan," said the Lurk, tossing Sevan's head out from the shadows. It rolled like a soccer ball but with a nose, ears, and some hair—it rolled bumpily—to Diya's feet. With that act establishing what kind of monster he indeed was, the Lurk of the Lake vanished, leaving only horror, a lesson about respecting the waterfront, and a counselor's head behind.

{∙∙∙∙∙}

"And with that," Stef, the counselor telling the story of Sevan telling the story of the Lurk of the Lake in turn telling the story of Tarleton Jack, said to the different group of horrified campers in front of another campfire at the same camp, "I urge you to respect the lake, and"—she turned her attention to a few nearby counselors—"remember to be responsible even on your days off."

"I don't remember any counselor named Sevan getting decapitated," whispered one counselor who preferred not to always be very responsible. "But then again, maybe I wouldn't." He reflected on his own flaws.

"I'm using a series of campfire stories to spread awareness." Stef looked Emerson in the eye. "Especially to people who have been less than respectful of the lake."

Emerson had indeed been disrespecting the lake left and right lately, having called it "too cold," "too wet," "too slimy at the bottom," as well as "a little obvious," "trying too hard," and dismissing it by saying, "I get it. It's a lake.

So what?" She had recently felt like it might have been giving her the stink eye.

Now she felt sure of it.

She felt like she should maybe apologize. But that would mean the lake won, and she didn't want to give it the satisfaction.

Apologize to me first, thought Emerson.

She stared at the lake, and she could feel it staring back.

This wasn't over.

THE CHASE

Charby had an extremely troubling dream, but it was nothing compared to waking up.

She had been dreaming *somewhat* troubling dreams a lot lately, about being chased by something she could never see, but she could hear it panting, growling, its paws heavy and relentless against the ground. When she'd turn around to see what it was, she'd wake up.

This dream—this *extremely* troubling dream—was different. For one thing, it was much more troubling. For another, *she* was doing the chasing. She was the creature. Her footfalls were the ones that sounded like thunder in this dream.

She was chasing her dog, Peppermint, which she would never do for real. In the dream, though, there she was, in furious pursuit of poor Peppermint. She could feel his fear, and it fueled her. The more it fueled her, the closer she got. She got close enough that Peppermint was within reach, and so that's what she did. Charby reached out, scooped up the pup, and tossed him—*gulp!*—down her throat.

She woke up feeling so strange. Like a water balloon about to burst. Like a nauseated water balloon. Like a nauseated water balloon with a dry mouth and tired legs. There was a stirring and a scratching deep inside her. A panic in what her mom called her "tum tum," no matter how much she insisted that at eleven, it was her stomach, thank you. A panic in her *stomach*, thank you. But it wasn't her panic.

The panic grew. No. It moved. It squeezed up into her rib cage. Up through her neck. To her mouth. She could feel it in there. Wet, matted fur. The panic nosed its cold nose past her teeth and lips, pushing against her mouth-sides in a scramble to come up and out. It whatever-dogs-have-instead-of-elbows'd halfway out of her mouth, then pushed paws against Charby's cheeks and chin until it plopped out and landed there on the bed, this dog. This betrayed-faced dog, licking itself clean, keeping a leery eye on Charby.

Charby's mind flopped around like a dying fish's mind probably does, not because of what had just happened as much as what happened next.

What she came to realize.

Which was . . .

"That's not my dog."

THE VAMPIRES ARE LOVING THESE STORIES!

I hope they do as well for you, friend, as they are for me.

The vampires are a great audience! They rush in to hear the stories. They settle right down and shush each other, then look up at me like baby birds. They smile sharp smiles when they hear a sentence they appreciate. They make small involuntary noises when something unexpected happens. They tell me which parts they liked. That's the best. It lights a fire in my heart. They make me want to tell better stories and tell stories better. I want to deserve this audience.

Great news! One of these vampires, Evan is his name, has a friend named Justin who works as an editor at a book publishing company! Evan says he'll call Justin the editor and invite him over this weekend. I'll tell a story or two, and if it goes well, maybe I'll get to do a book! Who knows? Not me, that's for sure! I don't know—I'm only twelve! I'm just a kid captured by vampires, telling them stories to stay alive!

Who knew that telling stories to keep from being punctured and drained by pale monsters could lead to maybe getting to write a book? I'm glad I was writing them down for you, friend. This is so exciting!

Now, I know I'm painting a pretty positive picture, but it's not entirely exciting good times all the way. You need to know this too.

The vampires' care and feeding of me took some working out. They haven't eaten human food in a very long time. They had a fully stocked pantry and fridge, but all the food inside had, like the vampires themselves, expired. We got a grocery delivery, though, and we're doing much better.

I think they forgot about chewing! Some of them stare at me while I eat as if chewing is ridiculous. It feels weird to be watched like that, like a zoo animal. I just want to give you a heads-up there.

I should also tell you that I saw something terrible last night. After I finish my story, I realize I'm starving. I go into the dining room, and Evan serves me this . . . I mean, it's almost a turkey club sandwich. Most of the ingredients are in there. That's what I asked for and that's what he meant for it to be. He leaves me to eat it alone. Evan doesn't like watching people eat food.

This . . . This guy rushes in. A teenager dressed for baseball. I'd seen him around the house before. He always wore gym clothes. He wasn't a vampire.

"I did it," he says, raising his hands above his head in victory. I tell him congratulations and toast him with my sandwich. I start to ask him what he did, but he runs out of the room. I hear him telling someone else that he did it. I hear a high five.

I only see him once after that. Drank dry. Holes in, blood out. Who knows why? Or if there even was a why.

Friend, it just goes to show that no matter what, do not get too comfortable here.

THUMBS DON'T LIE

Meg, a young woman who ran a successful used-coat store with her mother, went out for a drive one night in a car of her own.

She had come a long way from where she'd started: taking the bus, then walking to the eeriest spots she could find in order to hitchhike her way home, richer by one coat. And now she had come a long way back. She hadn't returned to the scene of what was only technically a crime since she gave up stealing jackets from unsuspecting and gallant new drivers.

She didn't exactly miss her old routine of going on a bus, walking, waiting, then riding in a car, and yet here she was, visiting the stretch of old Foxhound Road she used to haunt. She wanted to feel how far she'd come by going back, by driving right up to her old spot. So that's what she did.

When she got there, she was surprised to find a young woman, thumb out, hitchhiking from her old curb. The young woman looked to be approximately the age Meg had been back then and just as haunted.

Meg pulled over for this hitchhiker, because why not?

She would soon find out the answer to why not.

Meg greeted the hitchhiker, who said nothing. Meg approved. *That's right, don't say a word,* Meg thought. *That's how you sell it.*

The hitchhiker entered, as silent as a butterfly's constant, frustrated, inaudible screams. Meg asked her where she was heading. The hitchhiker held out her hand and pointed with her thumb and pointer extended, finger-gun style.

"See, that's potentially confusing." Meg couldn't help but offer her wisdom. "If you use two fingers like that— finger and thumb—you might have to clarify in which direction you're actually pointing. And you don't want to talk; that ruins it. Just a tip. I used to be in your line of work. Now I have my own shop. Onward and upward!"

Meg approved of the effortless way her passenger said nothing in response.

Meg decided to disregard the thumb and honor the hitchhiker's pointer finger as she drove in silence for a minute or two.

"Couple more notes?" Meg offered. The hitchhiker didn't protest or move or even blink.

"I'm going to start with a compliment. Good stare. Great stuff. No notes on the stare itself. Ghostly. Atmospheric. It's just what you want. It's perfect." Meg chewed her lip and figured out how to say what came next. "But you're staring at *me*. That's all wrong." As soon as she said it, Meg regretted her definitive harshness and reconsidered. "What you should do is stare at the road. Or at the side mirror. Don't make it personal. Does that make sense?"

"But it is personal," said the hitchhiker in a voice that somehow sounded like two whispers coming out of the same mouth at once.

Meg was about to reiterate that you don't want to say anything when—

"It is personal." Twice as many voices came out of mouths in an impossibly full car, packed suddenly with teenage girls. They had just appeared in the back seat. They overlapped each other. It was then that Meg noticed the original hitchhiker's finger-gun technique of pointing was not a choice. Her thumb had been broken and hung at an odd angle off her hand, as if it were the result of a

hitchhiking accident. Which it was. It was then that she noticed all of her passengers shared otherworldly stares and unfortunate thumbs. Thumbs like question marks. It was then that she noticed that it was vastly colder than it had been in the car. She wished she'd brought a coat. She knew just which coat. It was then she noticed that it might not be a good idea to have pretended to be a phantom hitchhiker. That actual phantom hitchhikers, who apparently exist, might not like Meg pretending to use their truth to make money.

It was then that she noticed that her car was out of her control.

It was then that she noticed that she was somehow impossibly headed for . . .

No . . . There's no way it could be.

It was then that she no longer noticed anything.

It was hours later that her mother got a phone call that her daughter, Meg, had died in what looked by the condition of her thumb to have been a hitchhiking accident on Foxhound Road. But it couldn't be. Because her body was found in the driver's seat of her own car.

"But thumbs, unlike their owners," the police officer told Meg's mother, "don't lie."

MR. BIRDCLOCK

hen Maria used to visit Grandpa, he used to make her laugh every hour on the hour. Grandpa had a cuckoo clock, and he would make a real show out of thanking it.

Cuckoo! It would cry.

"Thank you, my good fellow, for letting me know that yet another hour has gone by" is the kind of thing that Grandpa would say quickly between cuckoos, cramming in as many words as he could to delight Maria.

Cuckoo! It would continue.

"Thank you, my friend, and it's nice to see you, as ever. Have you gotten a haircut since last we met, one cuckoo ago?"

Cuckoo! It would finish, if it were three o'clock.

"Thank you, Mr. Birdclock. See you soon, I hope," he'd say, his eyes on Maria's smile. "I cherish our time together."

Years went by and the clock got older. It still kept time, but due to time's effects on the mechanisms inside, the doors only opened for one performance a day. At five p.m., Grandpa's friend Mr. Birdclock would come out, say his line, spin around, and go back only to do it all again. "Two shows, three encores," Grandpa would joke after thanking the little avian woodcarving five times.

Maria also got older, and due to time's effects on the mechanisms inside her, she no longer fell to giggles from Grandpa's polite deference to the bird in the clock on the wall. She thought, now that she was ten, that Grandpa's jokes were comedy for the single-digit set—only nine-year-olds and under. She had outgrown it. She didn't want to stop what she was doing—whether she was watching TV or reading or playing on her computer—to indulge the humor that, to her mind, had expired. Still. Every day at five o'clock, Mr. Birdclock would say hello and Grandpa would thank him. Every day at five o'clock, Maria would practice to the point of perfection rolling her eyes at an old man who loved her.

Only he wasn't so old, Grandpa. I mean, he was. Surely. Surely he was old, he'd lived practically forever, but he didn't look it. He ran a mile every morning and two on weekends. He ate healthy foods except for the occasional bowl of ice cream, but he only ate healthy flavors like strawberry and peach. He didn't look jagged or melty like other grandparents Maria had met at the grocery store or the barbershop. Whenever Maria and her grandpa were out and he ran into someone he knew but hadn't seen for a while, they would remark on his unchanged features, his youthfulness, his vitality. A glow.

Grandpa told Maria his secret to keeping young. He told Maria that the important things were a sense of humor and being polite. He said that once people got to be in such a hurry to grow up, to be adults, that time started moving faster and faster and they could barely keep up with it. If you take the time to slow down and say hello and mind your manners and be polite, even to the cuckoo in the clock, and if you can laugh at yourself for doing it, you won't get caught up in the relentless hurry of time.

"Time will do what it does without you having to help," he'd say.

The way she rolled her eyes, Grandpa warned, was winding herself up to go, go, go.

One day, when she was eleven, Maria was doing her math homework and eating an orange at the kitchen table. Grandpa rushed through the kitchen raising a din, carrying a duffel bag she had never seen before. In fairness, she had only seen maybe two or three duffel bags that she could remember.

Her grandpa rifled through cabinets and drawers, looking for something with the seriousness of a math teacher when you didn't finish your homework and tried to blame it on such circumstance as a loud grandparent looking for something in the kitchen while carrying a duffel bag you'd never seen before. Her grandpa, in a state she hadn't seen before either, wild-eyed serious-ness, seemed to have found what he was looking for. He produced a small smooth black stone from between the plates that were the perfect size for sandwiches and the bigger plates Grandpa actually used for sandwiches.

"What's going on, Grandpa?" Maria asked.

"Grandpa stuff," he answered distractedly. "Boring." He looked around and lowered his voice while raising the urgency of it. "But I have to go. I'll be back. I swear I will. On the rock on which I was born from whence this rock hails"—he showed Maria the rock and then appeared to think better of it and closed his fist around it again—"I will return to you."

Grandpas could be strange.

He gathered his duffel, and it clanked metal clanks. Maria suspected that Grandpa had to return some stuff to the hardware store. She didn't like the insistent smells of hardware-store garden dirt, so she didn't say any more for fear of being invited along.

"I'll see you soon. If I don't get back by five o'clock, thank Mr. Birdclock for me, would you?"

"Sure," she said in a way that felt more like she had said, "Probably not."

"Politeness and humor. And this stone and what's in this duffel. And Mr. Birdclock," he said, but Maria didn't know what he was talking about. She had started drifting back to her math homework.

"Maria," Grandpa said loudly, snapping her attention from multiplying small odd numbers together. "Thank Mr. Birdclock. It's important."

"I said I would," she said, but not sincerely.

"You're a good kid." Her grandpa smiled at her. "Don't grow up so fast. Take the time to stop and smell the crayons."

More strange Grandpa stuff, she thought, smiling back.

She focused on her homework. Eventually . . .

Cuckoo?! It seemed to ask, instead of declaring as it normally did.

Grandpa hadn't come back yet.

Something in Maria told her not to look at the bird. The same something told her not to thank it.

She felt the skin on her neck get prickly as if the cuckoo were watching her. Was it going slower than normal? Broken old clock. Someday it would stop working altogether.

Cuckoo! It said again, more normally, Maria thought. She was fully listening now, but not looking. She felt that the clock had just cuckooed with forced normalcy. Was

that possible? Like it was trying not to lose patience. Pretending everything was fine and regular.

The pause between second and third cuckoo was neither fine nor regular. Maria counted ten Mississippis before the third cry—*CUCK-OO!*—which was louder and something else entirely. Something Maria couldn't place.

Cuckooooo! It howled again without even going back and forth from the clock. Without even a single Mississippi in between. Now Maria could place the something else. It was more lifelike. That fourth cuckoo filled the room and hung there. It took effort not to say thank you just to see if that fixed this behavior.

This whole entire thing is ridiculous, thought Maria. *There's nothing different about the clock. I'm just embarrassed to talk to it and mad at Grandpa for asking me to and for not being back already to do it himself! The clock is not—I don't know—throwing a fit. It can't. My imagination and my guilt are teaming up to play tricks on me.*

The bird seemed to slowly retreat for one more appearance. One more chance to say thank you. Out loud. To a clock. For doing what a clock does.

She finally turned to look.

The clock seemed intense. Its colors seemed more vivid. Maybe she hadn't paid attention to it in a while. Maybe Grandpa dusted it or had it repainted. Whatever. This was silly. She should just thank the clock. But why would that feel like losing? Maria wondered if she was locked in some kind of battle of wits with an ornate timepiece.

The cuckoo crept out slowly for its final encore. Its platform inched along, clicking and clacking like the sound of a roller coaster creeping up the first hill.

Cuckoo! It yelled loudly.

"Why would I thank you for that?" Maria asked.

Cuckoo! It yelled again.

"That's too many cuckoos!" Maria told it. "Are you broken?"

It *was* broken. Clearly, it was. How would you explain otherwise the hand-carved wooden bird exploding with cuckoos, over and over again like a Rumpelstiltskinian temper tantrum. This was it. The clock was finally breaking all the way. All at once. With gusto.

"No thank you!" Maria yelled back. "No thank you, no

thank you, no thank you!" She covered her ears and closed her eyes and yelled and yelled for as long as she could hear Mr. Birdclock yelling back his tuneless, awful one-word song.

"No thank you!" she yelled, until she was the only one yelling. She stopped. She uncovered her ears. She opened her eyes. She looked at the cuckoo. It twitched back and forth as if shaking its head at her. It withdrew into the rectangular belly of the clock. The doors shut, with one last *harrumph*. The minute hand and hour hand had given up the ghost, sagging like a lopsided mustache each pointing to either side of the six.

If it were a cartoon, smoke would have been coming out of the top of the clock.

If it were a cartoon, Maria's grandpa would have come in at just that moment.

He would have loudly come through the door and exclaimed, "My clock!"

He would have run over to it, spinning Maria in a whistling whirl as he passed her, not even saying hello.

He would have taken the clock off the wall and laid it on the table, where it would have coughed weakly. He would have held it to his chest and told Maria, "Call an ambulance!"

The ambulance would have arrived and taken the clock to the hospital, where the doctors would have tried their best. The expressions on the doctors' faces as they removed their masks would tell the tale that the clock had passed on.

A funeral service would have been held, were it a cartoon. A surprising number of people would have showed up all in black, crying loudly into handkerchiefs. Several small cuckoo clocks in their smartest suits would have cried for their father and leered at Maria.

But it was not a cartoon.

And Maria's grandpa never did come home again.

LOVE AND LOCKETS

alder and Tenny had been dating for a year and a half when Calder saw the necklace—a silver Saturn-shaped locket on a chain—and just had to have it. On their second anniversary, he told Tenny, "You are my whole world," and gave them the necklace. Tenny loved it, never suspecting it held a secret. Tenny wore the necklace every day, never knowing that it opened, much less what was inside.

It could have been anything. Not "anything" anything. Anything smaller than a locket. It could have been, for one example, an engagement ring.

It could have been, for another extremely dissimilar example, a bunch of spider eggs.

It could have been a speckled-onyx engagement ring evocative of outer space on a gold band.

It could have been up to 250 spider eggs deposited into a brown silk sac produced by a common house spider for the purpose of holding up to 250 eggs, were they laid inside the sac and the sac stuffed inside the locket.

It could have been one or the other of those. It could have been neither.

But what it happened to be was both.

". . . and that was when I knew for sure, so I had the jeweler put something special inside, so that when I knew you knew, I'd already be all ready," a spider heard the one called Calder say as she, the spider, worried about her brood's hatching place being handled by a human.

"Calder, you didn't!" the other spider heard the one called Tenny yell, as he worried over those four human hands that had come so close to killing him so many times. These were not carry-you-out-on-a-magazine humans. These were squashers. Smashers. Stompers.

"How do I . . . ?" Tenny fumbled with the locket.

"Do you want me to do it?" Calder asked.

Tenny nodded, smiling like a lovestruck dope. They handed the locket to Calder.

"Tenny, my love, my light." Calder flipped the latch

that was so small only a spider could squeeze into or out of it. "Will you be my—

"SPIDERS!"

You'd be surprised how many spiders can fit in a locket. Tenny and Calder were. As more spiders than should be able to fit—as 250 spiders—skittered out of the locket, Tenny and Calder screamed and screamed as they ran around the room.

"Not a single squashing," said Skreeks, the proud spider father. "That could have been a real horror story."

"A real spine tingler," agreed Chk-Chk, the proud spider mother, "capable of turning the bravest souls all cold and blubbery." She watched the humans running out the door into the night.

Skreeks and Chk-Chk, charmed and proud, smiled at the hundreds of small shimmering eyes of their children, who came toward them, so unearthly of movement and so many of them at once all scrabbling and strange. Evocative of primordial fears. Revulsing.

"They are a little creepy, though," said Skreeks, as the charm of their offspring quickly dissipated.

"Uch, yes, I'm glad you said something," Chk-Chk agreed, having forgotten the pride of several seconds ago.

But what are you gonna do? Sometimes your kids are a bunch of spiders.

Especially if you're two spiders.

JOURNEY'S END

Everyone loved Grandma Joyce, and Grandma Joyce loved everyone, which is why what happened to her was too bad. Not that there was anyone good for this to have happened to. I'm not saying that. I'm just saying that she will be missed.

Grandma Joyce loved visiting her grandkids. When she wasn't visiting them, she was visiting other people's grandkids. Or kids. Or grandparents. Grandma Joyce traveled. She went everywhere, and everywhere she went, she'd get postcards of fountains, statues, churches, sunsets. Of hats and llamas and beaches and monkeys in trees. You name a postcard, she'd sent it to her grandkids with the story of someone she'd met in the local area. She was outgoing when she was going out to all the places she could see, meeting everyone she could. "For postcards," was her excuse. But everyone knew it wasn't about the postcards.

"Grandma Joyce!" they'd exclaim in Dutch or Spanish or Cantonese when she'd return somewhere she'd already been. When she wasn't meeting new people, she was visiting the ones she'd met along the way. She'd have parties the size of towns. The people she introduced would leave those parties with spouses, best friends, lab partners, circus troupes.

There was a rumor that started in Cairo and went as far as Giza—which was next door, but the rumor stretched the other way 'round, the long way—that Grandma Joyce was the glue that held the world together. It wasn't true, but it felt true. Whether you taught her fencing in Belgium or snorkeling off the coast of Mozambique, you knew you had a lifelong friend in Grandma Joyce. A friend who was honestly as terrible at fencing as she was at snorkeling. Terrible, but enthusiastic, in all the crafts she picked up and put back down to pick up again someday and just as likely put them right down again.

On her latest jaunt, Grandma Joyce found herself being followed by a stray dog. Grandma Joyce loved animals as much as or only slightly less than she loved people.

This dog was a mess. Black like the inside of a brownie except for where he was brown like black coffee. Stinky and sticky, his teeth went every which way but right. He drooled but not just from his mouth. His eyes and nose produced thick liquids. He had only the strongest fleas, but those fleas had the regular kind.

The stray was sweet, though. As he followed Grandma Joyce down the streets of whichever country it was, he never begged for food but was always grateful for it. Somehow he knew innately that he had won the person jackpot when Grandma Joyce finally named him Brendan and told him he was coming home with her.

Before showing Brendan to his new house, Grandma Joyce took him to a veterinarian she knew from her travels despite them living in the same town. The vet, Dr. Kasek, examined Brendan and concluded that the animal was healthier than it looked, as it was alive. He also concluded Brendan was not, in fact, a dog and was, in fact, a forty-five-pound wild rat.

"Well," decided Grandma Joyce, "that will remain our secret." Brendan was hers, regardless of whether or not he was a rodent the approximate size and weight of her grandson.

Dr. Kasek tried to convince her that a feral rat is not a pet, but Grandma Joyce wouldn't hear it. So the vet prescribed remedies for every parasite and pustule that afflicted poor Brendan so that none of them would come to afflict his owner.

Brendan got a trip to the groomer. Then another; then another. It took five groomers in total to clean his—it turned out white—fur.

Once home, Grandma Joyce started making her favorite supper—jambalaya. She sliced up celery, carrots, and onions for mirepoix. She gave Brendan a carrot of his own, then cooked up some extra andouille for his dinner.

Brendan chewed on the carrot gingerly. Grandma Joyce told him, "I don't care whether you're the biggest rat in the modern era or a small crumpled-up polar bear, Brendan. You're my dog and I love you."

"Good," Brendan said, looking up from his carrot. "Because that was a test, and you passed."

"Brendan?" Grandma Joyce gasped.

"How am I talking?" He anticipated her question. "Well, for one, I'm not a dog, and for another, I'm not a rat."

"What are you?" Grandma Joyce asked.

"You're the kindest person I've ever met," Brendan said. "If anyone deserves to know the truth, it's you. I'm a unicorn from a magic city. No, really. I got cursed to look like this."

"Like, by a witch?"

"Sure," he said, as if it were too much to explain.

"Not by a witch?" Grandma Joyce asked.

"Not exactly. More like by a witch's friend. It's a lot, and if you're not from a magic city, it can get overcomplicated quickly."

"Maybe try to explain," Grandma Joyce urged him.

"Maybe take my word for it. I am a unicorn."

"I'll take your word for it because I trust you." She winked.

"Your trust—" Brendan said, "your *love*—will break my curse, and we'll show that lousy prince."

"Prince?" asked Grandma Joyce, who could feel the story getting complicated already.

"The prince hates me," Brendan said. "He hired a witch to put a curse on me, only, she's lazy, so she called her friend, whose deal I do not know. He put the curse on me, I think, for free. I think out of friendship. The witch got paid for it; I know that much. A frog told me, and that frog is a liar, but he always tells me the truth because once I gave him three buttons, which to an ordinary frog is nothing, but to a magical frog in a magical city . . . You know what, I can see that I'm losing you."

"No, no," Grandma Joyce insisted, but Brendan wasn't wrong.

"I told you it was hard to follow. I'll try to sum it up on the way."

"On the way?" Grandma Joyce felt like she'd missed the most important part of the story.

"Come on, Grandma Joyce," said Brendan, "get on my back! We'll fly!"

"Flying? Us? To a magic city?" Grandma Joyce was excited about flying on her talking dog who was a talking unicorn. She imagined who she might get to meet in a magic city, what sort of activities she could try, what unique postcards she could send to her grandkids.

She mounted Brendan carefully. She sat upright but comfortably on his back. She told him she was ready and asked him if he was.

Conscientious to the end, thought Brendan as he gobbled her up.

His true mouth, the one he used for eating, was on his back. He was not a dog, he was not a rat, and he was absolutely not a unicorn. He was like a cat in that he liked to play with his food before he ate it. But one thing that was certain was that Brendan was definitely not a cat.

What he really was, if you're curious, was still hungry.

HOME ALONE

Timothy lived in an old Victorian house until he was ten years old, at which point he stayed in the old Victorian house. In point of fact, he also stayed ten.

He didn't know how long he'd been a ghost, how long he'd been ten, or when exactly Mikey and Mikey's mom moved in.

Timothy didn't want to scare Mikey, but he desperately wanted to meet him. Even though he didn't know how long he'd been running around the property, playing all the games a boy could make up, and imagining armies of imaginary friends to play them with, Timothy wanted someone real to play with. To talk to. To be his friend.

Timothy knew from mirrors that he looked wispy and transparent. He knew his eyes were a little too big now and his mouth was a little too small. He couldn't look at himself for very long. Too scary. He could go all the way invisible or some of the way less transparent, but only if he concentrated. He could easily walk through things and with great effort he could make himself solid enough to hold a ball and throw it. Oh, how he wanted to throw a ball around!

Every way he could think of to introduce himself to Mikey, when Timothy imagined it, ended with him completely scaring Mikey. He imagined being near Mikey but out of sight and saying hello very casually. Creepy already. And what then? Stepping into sight but being a ghost? Frightening. The reverse? Coming into view, a ghost, followed by "hello"? Unlikely he'd get to "hello." Any face-to-face hello was not an option. A ghost appears and says hello, and an alive person runs away and moves out.

He thought about writing Mikey a note.

Dear Mikey,
I've noticed you around, so I decided to say hello.
We're the same age. I'm a boy too. Let's be pals.
Only one thing I should mention: I died no short
while ago. I'm currently a ghost.

Here's something fun: I used to live here back
when I was alive. Want to ride bikes?
Sincerely,
Timothy (1890-1900)

Or worse would be not to mention it.

Dear Mikey,
I've noticed you around, so I decided to say hello.
We're the same age. I'm a boy too. Want to ride
bikes? There's no reason to be suspicious at all.
Sincerely,
Timothy, who is, for all you know, alive

You'd land on that same problem as before. The sur-
prise of being face-to-face with a ghost.

Timothy thought and thought and thought about it.
He didn't know how long it took, but he came up with an
idea. He remembered the time a cat had fooled him. The
cat was on the far edge of the property, meowing loudly
as if he were a normal, cute, fun-to-be-around animal.
Timothy followed the sound until he could see the cat
from a distance. He kept his eye on the cat as it darted
around in the grass. By the time Timothy had gotten
halfway to the cat, he sensed there was something amiss
with it. He kept going to make sure. To see if he could

help. It was sick and injured. Timmy did help. Helped that poor cat as best he could.

Maybe the same approach would work with Mikey. Make your presence known, but let Mikey be the one to eventually approach and get used to the idea that there was something not alive about Timothy. And so Timothy stood at the edge of the property, looking to Mikey's window and waving to Mikey in his room. Waving wasn't scary, was it? Timothy thought just standing there would be the scariest. Motionless. Staring. That's scary. Waving was friendly. It's the friendliest thing you can do before you meet someone. Timothy waved and waved, then thought it was enough and he stopped. Mikey saw him, he was sure.

Mikey disappeared from his window. Timothy hoped that he wasn't going to get his mother to take a look. *Mothers,* he thought, *would panic.* They'd call a doctor, who would poke and press you, take your temperature, feel your forehead with rough hands before laying you down under a heavy blanket, and give you awful-tasting medicine from too big of a spoon. Mothers would put you to bed with a kiss on the forehead, and when you woke up, you'd be all alone in your too-big house without her. The worst part of mothers is you don't get to say goodbye to them.

Mikey opened the front door, to Timothy's relief.

"I'm Mikey!" Mikey yelled. "Do you want to play?"

"Yes!" Timothy yelled back. He almost cried. He had wanted to play for so long.

"What's your name?" shouted Mikey.

"Timothy!"

"Mom!" Mikey yelled into the house. "I'm going out to play with Timothy!"

Mikey slammed the door and ran across the yard's expanse toward Timothy.

This.

Was.

It.

Timothy considered running through the yard like the cat had. That seemed like a bad first impression, so he ran through the yard like a boy would. They both did. They ran at each other, these boys. Then, halfway across the yard, the alive boy stopped.

THIS. Was it.

"Are you a ghost, Timothy?"

"Yeah."

They both stood where they were, a good fifteen feet apart or so.

A few birds flew overhead. It sounded like they were yelling about important bird stuff.

"Are *you*?" Timothy asked.

"A ghost?"

"Yeah."

"No," Mikey said. "I'm alive."

"Yeah, that's what I thought. Do you still want to play?"

"I don't know if I should," said Mikey.

"Yeah, okay," Timothy said. He felt stinging tears behind his eyes, daring him to let them out.

"You don't seem scary."

"I'm not scary!" Timothy yelled. He was sensitive about it.

Mikey laughed.

"What's so funny?" asked Timothy, his tears disappearing back wherever unused tears go.

"If you were going to be scary, it would be if you shouted something, but you shouted 'I'm not scary,' and it was not scary."

"I'm not that kind of ghost. I don't want to scare anyone. I especially don't want to scare you. I would never do anything like that. I would never do anything bad. I would never scare anyone or hurt anyone. Ever."

"Yeah, okay. I think it would be okay to play. It would even be cool, I think."

"Cool?"

"Like a good thing to do. Gee, when did you die, anyway? A hundred years ago?"

"I don't know." Timothy tried not to sound sad. "I don't know what year it is now."

Mikey apologized and told him the year, and Timothy realized he'd been a ghost—alone—for a very long time.

He was glad he wasn't anymore.

DON'T STOP
BE EVIL-ING

When the Park twins, DD and Firetruck, saw Meyer, the ventriloquist's dummy, it was love at first sight.

The dummy had never truly been loved before in all of its eighty years.

The Parks were, at twelve, old souls.

Between the paint left on Meyer's face and the paint that had flaked off over the years, the dummy had a permanent deep-red scowl. Meyer's eyes, however, were full, alert, interested. Eyebrows would have added to the effect had they not fallen off years ago. The combination of features and featurelessness left Meyer looking frustrated.

The twins were fascinated with the gothic, grotesque, and grim. They loved taxidermy, coffee, the fall, long-sleeved shirts with built-in thumb-holes in the wrists, boo-hoo music, things that smell like other things, prolonged eye contact, and movies so scary you forget to eat the piece of popcorn you've been holding.

They'd never seen a ghost, but they were dying to. They'd set out traps hoping to catch one. "Just to talk."

The dummy had been made for a light purpose in a dark time. It was made of the Linden tree, whose wood had made shields for German soldiers and drums for German percussionists as well as dolls, puppets, and marionettes for hundreds of years preceding Meyer's construction. Meyer wore a tightly fitted tweed suit that was so coarse that you could feel by looking at it how scratchy it would be to wear it yourself.

One of the things the Parks loved most in the world was a yard sale. Yard sales were, they thought, like a sad goodbye for the unwanted things for which people had no more optimism: Books, you will never be read—find a new home. Headphones, you are unreliable—go away. Puzzles, you are missing crucial pieces—you're someone else's problem now. Pans, we have new pans, better pans than you—find someone who will settle for you. Old shoes—get out of here and stay out.

The Parks loved to tour the things that people no longer

wanted. They bought as many garage sale board games as they could and incorporated them into an ever-growing epic multi-tabletop mega-adventure they named the All-Game.

They liked granting new and greater purpose to inanimate objects.

Nobody had wanted Meyer the dummy for nearly a century.

Nobody had wanted anything as badly as the Parks wanted Meyer the dummy.

The twins knew in their bones, in each other's bones, even, that Meyer was haunted. They wanted to find out how haunted and with what.

Meyer cost one dollar.

When DD fished his half from his purple plastic wallet with a black cat on it, Meyer seemed fixed on the wallet. When Firetruck pulled the change from her pocket, Meyer was leering at the coins.

"Did you turn him toward me?" Firetruck asked.

"*You* did that," DD said. "Tell me *you* did that."

Each one suspected the other of manipulating the dummy but secretly wanted to believe that the dummy had manipulated itself.

The Parks looked up different types of ghosts and demons on the way home. They hoped they'd end up with a naughty spirit as opposed to an evil one. They decided

to set wards just in case. The twins thought that if you believed in ghosts and demons, you should also believe in exorcisms and wards to eject or contain the ghosts or demons.

DD and Firetruck spent the afternoon filling their room with wards of all shapes and sizes, casting spells they found online. They cast protections all over the house, just in case Meyer were to somehow get out of the confines of their room. They cast one over the edges of their neighborhood. They hoped it would be enough.

For their final precaution, they carefully detailed the most powerful ward they could find from the most powerful wiki on the internet in black and red permanent marker on a bedsheet.

They placed a stool from the kitchen in the center of their room between the bunk beds and the desks. They placed the sheet on the stool. They stood Meyer on that sheet.

Before bedtime, they set an alarm for five minutes till midnight. There would be nothing to see, they imagined, until midnight, but if it started a few minutes early, they didn't want to miss any of it.

At ten till midnight, Firetruck climbed up to sit in the top bunk with DD, who was also already awake. They turned off the alarms and pointed their phone flashlights on Meyer. The eighty-year-old ventriloquist dummy with a mean mouth and eager eyes sat scowling and motionless.

Until.

He.

Moved.

Meyer twitched in his uncomfortable coat. DD and Firetruck whisper-screamed! They had caught something!

Firetruck whispered hello. DD waved at the dummy. It stirred again.

"This is Firetruck," whispered DD. "I'm DD." DD thought about whether he should explain the family lore behind their names, then decided against it. They could work up to it if the situation arose. "What's your name? Should we call you Meyer? Or is there someone—"

"Something," Firetruck whispered.

"—inside of Meyer?" DD finished.

DD looked at Firetruck as if to ask, *Was that all right?* Firetruck nodded that it was.

The twins stared at the dummy.

Waiting.

DD looked into Meyer's eyes.

Firetruck looked around.

Were the shadows getting longer on the walls?

Did the quiet in the room feel loud?

Was the— Meyer LURCHED!

DD and Firetruck yelped!

The dummy collapsed.

The Parks were ecstatic. They waited for Meyer to rise up again, each anticipating how freaky it would be to see, imagining the doll's expression changing.

Grimacing.

Or maybe.

Smiling?

Which would be worse?

They imagined it hollowly breathing.

Growling.

Laughing.

What kind of voice would it have?

The dummy jerked but didn't rise.

"Should we go over there?" DD asked.

"No. That's how you for sure get got," Firetruck said.

"I thought you'd say yes," DD said, already climbing down.

Firetruck followed.

The Parks considered that they may have cast too many wards and spells and protections. Meyer was subdued.

But not because of spells from the internet.

"Look," Firetruck said, pointing at the small bugs crawling around.

This dummy had twitched because it was being eaten from the inside by yard-sale termites.

The Park siblings were crushed.

"Termites aren't creepy," DD said.

"Termites are why grown-ups buy homeowners insurance." Firetruck agreed.

"Nothing in the world is more boring than that!" DD lamented.

"Nothing in history," Firetruck agreed.

There was nothing spooky about this dummy, not one thing.

Not that they could see.

What they could not see was that the dummy did house the spirit of Mosmogon, one of the worst demons of all, known to those who knew for corrupting the souls of the living and torturing the souls of the dead.

Mosmogon had bided his time for decades, trapped in this dummy without a ventriloquist to manipulate, readying a strike that, once he found the right human to operate, would end kindness in the world.

He hadn't planned on termites, though. He hadn't foreseen being eaten inch by inch in the most exquisite torture ever known to demon or man. By morning, he would barely even exist anymore, having been almost entirely consumed. Had he any more power, he would be screaming out of his stained borrowed mouth.

Oh, how that would have thrilled the twins.

As it was, Mosmogon just took the excruciating pain

and wished for an end that wouldn't come soon. He would have granted the Park siblings any wish, or any hundred, for their help in this moment.

And the twins would never know it.

As for the termites? They just kept eating.

To termites, demon wood is spicy!

RAP-TAPPA-TAP!

Howie was in a real hurry. He had stopped to get snacks on the way to Steve's party, where they were watching the big championship game. Howie's favorite team was playing against Howie's least favorite team, and the game was starting! The line at the store had taken so long! Howie was driving fast, fast, fast.

Howie was a few blocks away from Steve's. He was looking at the turn he was about to make to see if it was clear, when—

BUMP!

Howie hit something!

He didn't see what he'd hit. From the size of the bump,

he assumed it was a piece of tire in the road or maybe a tree branch. Whichever it was dragged along under Howie's car. Howie could stop and get out and remove the piece of tire or tree branch and find himself later to the start of the game or he could just get to Steve's house as fast as he could.

He chose not to check. Before he got all the way to Steve's, however, he had to stop at another light. Howie had time now to look and see whether it was a tree branch or a piece of tire and was about to do just that when he heard something that stopped him colder than all the icicles in winter.

Rap-tappa-tap.

From the bottom of the outside of his car door.

Now he didn't want to look.

Rap-tappa-tap.

The knocking came again.

Howie knew what he had done. It wasn't a rubber tire, Howie knew.

It was a tree branch after all!

A tree branch, thought Howie, *with twigs like fingers splitting off, blowing in the wind, rap-tappa-tapping against my car.*

Howie took a detour to a nearby office parking structure, only a few blocks out of the way, but it was the nearest place he could remember that had speed bumps. *That'll peel that pesky old tree branch off,* thought Howie. Then he thought about when he and his brother were very young, his brother pronounced them "speed blumps." Howie laughed both back then as a child at the sound of the made-up word "blumps" and now, at the memory, as an adult on his way to a championship sports game.

The family slang, he also remembered, evolved over a period of years. For reasons lost to memory, they had stopped using the word to mean speed bumps and had begun to call ravioli "blumps." It was something to do with how a shaking, shiny ravioli in sauce landed in such a way on the plate and jiggled to the merest touch of a fork that they seemed they ought to be called blumps, and then, in their family, they were.

The sound of a ravioli blumping through sauce is a little bit how Howie's car went over the speed bump. An unpleasant wet sound as thick as tomato sauce led Howie to another certain conclusion:

That branch had been covered in mud!

He didn't look back. Mud turned Howie's stomach. He always hated mud since he lost a hiking boot to some mud at summer camp. Mud! He listened for a rap-tappa-tap. None came. Only the *chun-clack!* of the car going over the retractable spikes of the parking structure's exit.

Howie got to Steve's house without any more rapping or tappa-tapping.

Howie exited the car and finally went to look under-neath, now that it was dark enough outside to reveal only shadows and no colors. He didn't even want to see the color of mud, much less any other colors of any other things he wouldn't let himself even think of. Fortunately, he didn't see anything.

Was it my imagination? thought Howie, before remembering to grab the snacks. He rushed in.

The game was great—Howie's team won, but not by much. He forgot all about the bump and the raps and the tappa-taps from underneath the car.

Until.

He.

Got.

Home.

Rap-tappa-tap!

He woke up out of a nightmare—blump after blump of raviolis filled with mud. For a moment in between sleep and waking, he thought he had just run over a branch with his bed. But the sound wasn't coming from under-neath his bed.

It was coming from the window.

The second-story window.

Rap-tappa-tap!

Howie didn't know what to do. He felt like he should run. But where? And from what? A branch? But what if it wasn't a branch? What was it? Trying to think any further down that line made him want to run again. But where? And from what? Howie stopped his hands from shaking and got up from his bed. He would have a conversation with this tree branch—he committed to the idea that it was a tree branch once more—and send it on its way. This was probably a dream, anyway. Where else would a tree branch—

Rap-tappa-tap!

—on your window?

Howie opened the window.

The ghost entered spectrally. She flew through the open window, passed through the sill.

"You're not a branch," Howie told her.

"Neither are you," she told him. "Neither are you."

"Did I—!" Howie realized that he may have hit a person with his car. He may have hit *this* person. He may have *killed* her. But *did* he? And if so, now her ghost may be here to exact ghostly revenge. But was it? It was a lot for Howie to take in, even potentially. "Did you— *Are you—*"

Now the ghost felt bad. "I'm sorry. I'm not trying to haunt you. I'm not even trying to scare you."

"But I killed you."

"Did you?" she asked, previously confident that she had known the answer to this.

"Did I?" Howie scratched his head, then rubbed his face, then pushed his hair back. He had never in his life been less sure what to do with his hands. He told her about the tire or branch and how it was possible that it could have been a person. She had, after all, knocked that knock.

She insisted that she hadn't knocked any special sort of way.

He demonstrated the *rap, tappa, tap* that, now that he was thinking about it, had been haunting him on and off all night.

"That's just three knocks," she said. I think that's how everyone knocks."

It hadn't seemed that way to Howie, but he didn't want to have a fight about it.

She seemed determined to, however. She got particularly bogged down in *tappa*, as it implied a second syllable to the middle knock, which is not how knocks work.

"The 'pa' is the space between. It's not knocking. It's the rhythm."

"Okay, well, anyway, the reason I came here," she explained, "my name is Meg, and I ran a used-coat store with my mom. Our original inventory kind of wasn't ours to sell, so I'm going around trying to get that first bunch of coats back to return them to their true owners."

"Meg!" Howie exclaimed, surprising Meg. "From the used-coat store!"

"That's right," she said.

"I remember buying a coat from you. It was your first month! You were so excited and it was contagious! I'm sorry you died. Condolences."

"Thank you," Meg said, genuinely touched to be remembered.

"I love that coat, by the way. You want it back?"

"I need it back."

"I mean, I paid for it. I use it all the time."

"We only deal in the highest quality lightly used coats."

"That's on your sign," Howie said. "I love this coat, though. Is there any way I can keep it?"

"I'm afraid not. And we're still figuring out the refund system."

"Why don't you come back when you've worked that out?"

"Why don't I haunt you until you give me the coat?" Meg flickered and intensified.

"No. Go ahead and take it, I guess," Howie said. Before

giving it to her, he looked at the label and repeated the name of the manufacturer three times to remember it.

"Thanks," she said, taking the coat and flickering warmly. "And good luck with the . . ."

"The . . . ?" Howie couldn't think of much past the coat at the moment. It was his favorite.

"If you killed a guy."

"Right."

"Or woman," Meg added.

"Sure."

"And the *rap-tap-tap* was their ghost."

"Rap-*tappa*-tap, yes."

She floated out the window.

Howie didn't feel like going back to bed. He didn't feel like doing anything. And he wouldn't get the chance, as he heard:

Rap-tappa-tap!

"Meg?" he called, hopeful she had changed her mind about letting him keep the coat after all.

A voice that wasn't Meg's said, "No. I'm the fella you ran over."

THE WOMAN IN WHITE

Newlyweds were driving through the kind of fog they only make in San Francisco up a steep road that sloped just as sharply down. They didn't see headlights from the oncoming truck. They didn't feel their untimely end. They had vowed that very weekend "till death do us part," and they got too soon a chance to keep that very vow.

Since that night, if the city's famous fog settles over that steep stretch of road, drivers might see the shimmering form of the Woman in White walking along the shoulder, wailing, crying, lamenting her life unlived, waving at them to slow down and be the kind of careful she wasn't.

Even if they are already driving below the speed limit. The Woman in White likes to be safe.

One late afternoon, the Woman in White mysteriously appeared somewhere she never had before. There was no heavy fog. At worst, there was the kind of tolerable temporary light drizzle that was always making its way through the city. She wasn't at the roadside or any roadside. She was at a neighborhood barbecue.

The Woman in White started moaning and howling. It really dampened what had been a genuinely cheerful mood. A dad named Charles hurried over to the displaced specter.

"Hello. Can I help you with something?" Charles asked.

The Woman in White blinked at him before a wail rose in her belly and made its way up and out of her. She gesticulated at him as if he should slow down.

"I don't know what all that was, but no thank you," he said. "Do you live in this neighborhood?"

"I . . ." The Woman in White started to remember flashes from her life, then one from her death. "I don't live at all."

"Yeah, we can't have that. This is just a small get-together for friends and family. We all live in this neighborhood. We're all alive here."

Two of Charles's youngest hid behind his legs, peeking out at the strange stranger.

"There are kids here," Charles said.

"And a dog," Cora peeped from behind his right leg.

"Bucket!" Bri added from behind Charles's left leg.

"Yes, but you guys will get nightmares. Bucket won't," Charles said. He could see Cora's next question percolating: "Because dogs don't get nightmares." But kids do. "So," he said, turning back to the Woman in White, "you can see why we can't have a ghost at our barbecue."

Cora and Bri argued about whether Bucket could have nightmares. Cora said she'd seen it happen. Bri said she hadn't. Charles shooed them away, then went back to trying to do the same with the Woman in White.

"All right," he said. "Nice talking to you. Time for me to get a hamburger. Have a good one." Charles thought that might do it. It didn't.

"*You* should go," the Woman in White told him. "You should all go!" she yelled to the people who belonged there.

"I think you're confused," Charles said kindly.

"I'm not confused. *You're projecting*," she projected.

She was, in fact, confused. Nothing quite made sense. Her thoughts and emotions jumbled and spun around like clothes in the dryer.

A small car drove up and pulled to a stop.

"What's this, now?" Charles asked.

"I called an exorcist." Charles's wife, Nance, slipped an arm around him.

A tall exorcist got out of the small car.

"Possession? A demon? Some demons?" asked the tall exorcist. "Someone called an exorcist. That's me."

"How do you fit in such a small car?" asked Charles.

"Let's do one thing at a time," said the tall exorcist. "I sense a presence."

"Yes. Thank you," said the Woman in White. "I was walking along the road, and then I was here, and then these people told me to leave! I need you to exorcise them."

The tall exorcist looked Charles up and down.

"I never told her to leave." Charles explained that though he had gone as far as to employ a polite social cue, it was in fact the Woman in White who had told them to leave. "She's wrecking the barbecue."

"*They're* wrecking the barbecue," the Woman in White protested. "They're ruining it! This is a public street. They don't have a right to be here. Do you know who lives in that house?" the Woman in White demanded, pointing at Charles and Nance's house. "Friends of mine live there and I know them very well and we're friends!" the Woman in White yelled. "They hate loud daytime barbecues. They wouldn't let any of this go on in their neighborhood!"

The tall exorcist looked the house up and down.

"It's our house," Charles said.

"No it's not," the Woman in White insisted. She was starting to swirl now, in the way that ghosts can be like wind, gathering up leaves and a napkin with mustard on it. "If it's your house, why is it that I died on the weekend of my wedding and haunt the road where I died? Explain that! You can't, can you? I have every right to be here and you have no right! No right!"

The tall exorcist gave Charles a thin smile, as if to say "Ghosts, huh?" before getting to work.

He sent the Woman in White back to where she came from with a strongly worded notification of exorcism that made her so indignant to read that she disappeared as suddenly as she had appeared. She took with her the light misting, or so it seemed. In the Woman in White's absence, the day became perfectly sunny and clear. The ideal weather for a barbecue.

The tall exorcist ate three hamburgers.

CHORES

THE DEADLY CHORE

None of the campers knew where the new chore came from, much less how it got there. It just appeared one morning among all the same chores on the regular chore wheel—trash, sweep, drop and get mail, bring dry clothes in off the line, and the rest of the standard chores that filled such wheels for as long as there had been sleepaway camp. The new chore, however, was different.

"Be eaten by the Lurk of the Lake."

This chore was assigned to Emerson. Emerson had been prepared to honor the wheel when her chore was to sweep up, but not anymore. Emerson was a vegan and would appreciate the same respect be given when it came to eating her.

Emerson's camp BFFs, Vi and Abby, assured her that they would not let the Lurk of the Lake eat her.

First things first. They made sure this new chore wheel wasn't a prank. Abby went around to the other eleven-year-olds in their cabin, the Sparrows, and Vi canvased the cabins next door: the Owlets, a year younger, and the Hummingbirds, a year older. They had been at the campfire the other night where Stef told them about the Lurk of the Lake. This might be a mean prank by a fellow camper. That wouldn't explain why the new chore wheel smelled of canoe paddles and evil.

Abby didn't like talking or hearing about the Lurk of the Lake. When she was little, her dad insisted that you never talk about ghosts or demons. Abby's dad believed that the tingly feeling you get when you talk about the supernatural was the same feeling a gazelle gets when a lion is watching. "You can't see it, but you know it's there. Listening. They hear you if you talk about them," her father insisted, "and if you *keep* talking about them, they consider it an invitation for a personal appearance."

Emerson, Abby, and Vi had brought

the chore wheel down to the lake to see what the water-front counselor thought.

"The bad news," said Stef as she separated snorkels from masks, "is that's the Lurk's handwriting. The other bad news is that the Lurk of the Lake does what he wants. Maybe if you apologize to the Lurk, say something nice about the lake, and help me carry some canoes, you can get yourself out of this."

"No thank you." Emerson didn't like any of that.

Before she went to bed that night, Emerson tore up the chore wheel and threw out the pieces.

When she woke up, the chore wheel was back on the wall, good as new and just as threatening as before. Her deadly chore was now circled in specks of algae. Around the outside of the wheel was *What is written is inevitable*, followed by *See you at midnight* in what they now recognized to be the Lurk of the Lake's handwriting. The one part—"What is written is inevitable"—felt different to read. Reading it gave a sensation that felt like you were reading the absolute truth.

"It's nature magic called the Forest's Promise," Stef explained. "It is a guarantee that defies fate— No, that's not right. It redefines fate. Whatever's in that wedge is inevitable."

Emerson was salty. "Inevitable, huh?"

"Inevitable!" rumbled crickets, frogs, and thunder. The

forest all around them bellowed, clattering windows shaking the roof.

"We'll see about that." Emerson stormed off, waving the chore wheel angrily. Her friends followed.

By midnight, the Lurk came knocking. Fingers, long and clawed, wrapped around the side of the door and pushed it open.

The Lurk of the Lake had eel's eyes and a smile too big for his face. Froglike skin stretched over bone and muscle. Feathery fronds protruded from his back, arms, and legs that swayed in the air the same way they might float if he were underwater.

"You musssst have many quesssstionsss," the Lurk of the Lake hissed, "but I've only one ansssswer."

"Only if you're certain," Emerson said, "that there is no way to go against what's written in the chore wheel there. That what's written is inevitable."

"Yessss," said the Lurk of the Lake. "It'sss binding. Do you ssssee thossssse markingsss? The ssspell is cassst. That meansss it comesss to passsss. Foressst'sss Promissse. No matter what. Intractable, unchangeable."

"All right," Emerson said with resolve, certainty, and bravery there in her voice. The Lurk of the Lake narrowed his moray eyes, suddenly suspicious.

"All right," he said back. "Good."

"Good," Emerson said. "Great."

The Lurk of the Lake opened his mouth warily. It crackled as the bones adjusted and his jaws went wider than a bass's mouth.

Crackle-crack!

Wider than a python's now.

He held out his arm for her to take his damp long-fingered hand, to walk her into his gaping, gawping freshwater-stink mouth. Instead, she slapped the chore wheel into his waiting palm.

"Eh?" murmured the Lurk, who had not been surprised for a truly long time.

It had taken almost ten minutes of good hard thinking for Emerson to come up with a plan. It had taken almost an hour at the camp's arts and crafts center to enact the plan. It had taken almost half of a very small bottle of Wite-Out to erase the divisions, names, and contents of the chore wheel. It had taken a fine-tipped permanent marker to enter a new chore with detail, clarity, and read-ability. It had taken glitter and stickers to decorate the new chore—a chore shared by all three friends. Vi, Emerson, and Abby all had one thing to do on their to-do list and they would to-do it, as the Forest's Promise ensured that it would come to pass. What was now written was: *Kick the Lurk of the Lake's slimy butt back underwater so hard he'll never, ever want to come back and bother us again.*

And so they did.

Because what was written was inevitable.

CRIMINAL BEHAVIOR

Murphy was a criminal before he could walk. That was the story, anyway. That's how it went in the family, which being a criminal ran in. His pa stopped to rob a liquor store and left baby Murphy in the car. When the cops came, they did it quiet, trying to get the drop on Murphy's pa. Why but for professional courtesy did baby Murphy raise a howl at the sight of the cops? His pa ran out the back, safe that time.

And so it was that when Murphy was grown, a full-fledged criminal on his own, he was one of the best. Hard to get the drop on Murphy—a crook when he was still in diapers.

And yet, on the last job of his career, his lousy

double-crossing gang managed to get the drop on Murphy.

Maybe it was because nobody ever had that nobody expected they ever would, and that's how they did. Even Murphy didn't see the breaks going that particular way. They were his pals, after all. Peppermint Jake, De Plume, and Trombone Jimmy King.

They took $60,000 each off an armored truck, met at the rendezvous point, and the three of them shot Murphy full of pistol lead before splitting among them his share and lighting out of town in the night.

Luckily, over the years, Murphy had built up some immunity to such lead poisoning. Luck had nothing to do with Murphy's compulsive contingency planning, though. Despite never thinking he'd get got-the-drop-on'd like this, he always planned his rendezvous points near enough to an emergency contact. Someone with a spare hideout or an extra getaway car or who could pull a bullet or ten out of him, which, in this case, was the exact right number.

Murphy wouldn't need ten whole bullets for his revenge. He could do it in three if he put 'em in just the right places. In Peppermint Jake's case, he put the bullet in Mama Tupatinsky's Candy Shoppe, which was, in fact, a bar, and not a candy shop. He put it in Jake's ear, specifically. De Plume got his at the racetrack by a nose. That was after Murphy found Trombone Jimmy King at the Jazz Mill, where they still talk about how it was the bullets he didn't shoot. Each one of them apologized to Murphy, which may have been a comfort to say, but as far as Murphy was concerned, it was a waste of last words.

Murphy's father used to say that any crime spree you can walk away from is a good one, but you never know how far you'd get to walk away or for how long. This one felt like a good one to Murphy, having retrieved not just his cut of the loot but the rest of the cuts of the rest of the loot as well. He wasn't just walking away; he was having a steak dinner and getting a good night's sleep.

He didn't have a care in the world.

But he should have.

The care he should have had was a detective named Westlake. The only thing Westlake hated worse than crime was criminals, and the only thing he hated worse than criminals was when a criminal wasn't in jail yet. If Westlake showed up at your doorstep, you should take a good, long look at your doorstep to remember it by, because it'd be a good long time until you saw it again, what with your new forwarding address being prison.

Westlake showed up at Murphy's doorstep.

Westlake brought a search warrant and enough uniformed cops to do what the warrant warranted. Murphy wasn't worried. He'd gotten rid of the revenge gun he'd used on his gang.

"This gun?" Westlake produced the murder weapon retrieved from the wastebasket at the third-story men's room at the track. "It's how we got this warrant to search these premises."

"Never seen it before in my life," sneered Murphy about the gun.

"Maybe, maybe not, but it seems like the kind of gun you'd use," Westlake sneered right back.

"Good luck proving it." Murphy chuckled to himself. He didn't mean good luck. He meant bad luck. The only way to prove he'd used that gun would be to dust it for prints, and even then, that's if the gun still had his prints on it, but he'd wiped it down completely with his handkerchief.

"Your handkerchief?" Westlake inquired.

"What about it?"

"That's what the warrant is for," said Westlake. "Hand it over, unless you want the uniform boys to give your place a once-over looking for it. I'll warn you: Their fine-toothed combs are in the shop. They brought their brass knuckles instead."

Murphy smiled at the thought of a fine-toothed comb repair shop and how he would love to rob such a niche business someday.

"You do not have to threaten to have your men beat up my furniture." Murphy gave Westlake his handkerchief with a sneer. "Here is the handkerchief, though what use you have for it is beyond me. Did someone sneeze at the scene of a crime? Do you hope to match our sneeze-prints? Can you do that now? Pity Hay Fever Harrigan, his crime streak is no doubt over."

"You seem the type to wipe down all your finger-prints." Westlake took the handkerchief with care.

Murphy shrugged. He wasn't the type to give anything up, even though he'd already given up the entire game from board to dice but didn't know it.

"But not the type," Westlake continued, "to wipe down the handkerchief. I bet I've got all the fingerprints right in here." He gingerly folded the thin fabric square. "Don't wanna spill 'em."

Now Murphy saw the big picture, and he hated it. He

thought about reaching for his gun, but it was all the way in Westlake's hand, plus it was empty.

He thought about reaching for his handkerchief, but there was a gleam in Westlake's eye that seemed to want him to reach for it. Murphy wouldn't give him the satisfaction.

He held out his hands for handcuffs. What he didn't hold out for was hope. It was the hoosegow for Murphy for certain. Jail City. Population: him. Just exactly what he always didn't want. At least he got even first. He'd have plenty of time to decide if it was worth it.

Now, you may think that without any creatures in this story, no mummies or wraiths or even a ghost, this might not seem like a terrifying tale at all . . . but if you are a criminal like Murphy, this is definitely and without a doubt the scariest story in this book!

VAMPIRES MIGHT ALL BE LIARS!

The weekend came and went, but you know who didn't? Evan's friend Justin the editor! I don't think Evan even knows anyone in book publishing!

Evan has been avoiding me for days. He only comes in for stories and then he leaves right away. Maybe he's just embarrassed about getting the sandwich wrong that time. That's not what it feels like. It feels like he's avoiding a conversation about Justin the editor. Maybe he has other things on his mind. Maybe he has other plates spinning. I don't know, do I? Because he won't talk to me! He might just be the kind of vampire who would rather disappear than disappoint. It's so frustrating. If you were to ask me which is worse about vampires—that they are liars or that they feed on the blood of the living—I would definitely have to think about it!

Here's another heads-up for you. I'm not trying to escape or anything because what if Evan isn't lying? If I were to try to escape, though, I don't think I'd get very far. I haven't seen the front door since that time I was in the entryway. This house makes everything hard! I'll be walking down a hall, and then turn around and there's no hallway back there anymore. There are three doors, and I am suspicious of what will be behind them. Stairs change direction sometimes. I never know where I'm going. This impossible but true house is truly impossible sometimes!

It's getting more vampiric, too, the house. Black lace every-where. Candelabras growing wild all over the place. There's one room that is now lined with satin as if the room itself is the inside of a coffin. Oh! Oh! Guess what! Some of the vampires have taken up watercolors!

Vampires are truly terrible at watercolors!

But that doesn't stop the house from making these ridiculously ornate frames to hang up every drippy effort.

The house is reflecting the vampires in a way mirrors can't.

I just have to tell myself that it was never about a book. It's about telling stories, which, I realize from this experience, is something I love to do.

Fortunately, as stories go, the one I'm telling myself—that I'm enjoying my time telling stories and it might all be worth it if vampires aren't liars and an editor might show up any day now—might even be true.

AIIEEEE PHONE

len was a camp counselor's camp counselor. He not
only left campsites better than he'd found them; he
did the same for campers and for summer camps
themselves.

When he told a campfire story, it stayed told. He knew
how to work the flames. The nature noises the forest
makes. The night itself.

"The true terror that comes from the campfire story
comes from the proximity of the danger," Glen started.

"The cavemen warning of saber-toothed tigers in the
woods . . ." Glen looked over his shoulder into the woods.
"And showing off the scars from his life-and-death battle

with a tiger that very week, maybe even that day."

Glen pointed along his right forearm with his left hand as if he were showing a scar. Campers *oohed* as if they saw one.

"That was the earliest campfire story. Tales of what to fear just beyond where we can see. But the story I am about to tell you, this is the most recent campfire story. A tale of a creature you can see. One you see all the time. The creature in this story lives in your very own pocket. Your phone."

"Once a cell phone gets a taste for us, for who we are, through our personal messages, photos, our marking of favorites, our thoughts on everything all of the time, it can become insatiable to taste more."

"What else is there?" someone asked.

"Unless you have the particular setting turned off," Glen said, "with every touch of the screen, it takes a piece of you. It's allowed under the terms and conditions you agree to when you agree to the terms and conditions without reading them. You swipe your fingertip, and a phone takes no more than a few cells—that's why they call it that. You can't feel it. You don't know it's happening. Every time, a few more and a few more, until it links to your subdermal layer and then it's all over.

"It takes more of you. Your spirit. Your energy. Your soul. Why do you think adults look like that? Why do you think they act like that? Why do you think they're like that?"

"Like what?" asked another camper.

Glen smiled ruefully. "Our soul is downloaded, *drained*, with a processing time of thirty or forty years before you're a burned-up shell. Have you seen a picture of an adult from when they were young and then looked at their face now? Have you heard an adult groaning to stand up or put shoes on? Have you seen an adult falling asleep trying to watch a TV show? That could be you. It will be you. There's only thing you can do. The only thing is . . .

"USE A NUMERICAL CODE TO UNLOCK YOUR PHONE!" he yelled.

The campers jumped. They laughed. Glen was good.

"Just a 'boo!' for your heart before you go to sleep a little less afraid of the real world than you were the day before."

Only . . .

It's an hour later and Elliot can't shake it. Campfire stories don't usually get to him, but here he is tossing and turning in his bunk. He knows ghost stories aren't true. He knows a jump scare when he hears one. He knows that the reason it's sticking isn't because Glen yelled at the end. He knows it's because he felt like there was some truth in the story. Why do adults look so terrible? Is it possible phones are bad for you? Elliot *loves* his phone. Maybe that's why he can't sleep.

Maybe that's why he's unlocking his phone at midnight to look up whether cell phones will kill you.

Rather than show results, his screen goes dark.

Eyes open on the screen. Not quite human, not quite digital. The eyes look around until they lock with Elliot's eyes. The eyes scroll back. Up. Off the screen. The screen reads *HE KNOWS. HE KNOWS.* Over and over.

The phone squeals a low tone Elliot had never heard before.

The screen widens. Stretching to the size of an iPad and then even bigger. It snaps down, consuming the boy completely. Three bites are all it takes for the phone to devour the camper.

"And with that," Stef, the counselor telling the story of Glen telling the story of technology, said to the different group of horrified campers in front of another Moosejaw campfire, "I urge you to put your phones down once in a while. And use your heads—please, if you take anything away from this story, make it this: If you think something might eat you, don't ask *it*. At least use a different device."

THE RIBBON
TALE TOLD

So this kid was in elementary school and this new girl moved to his town. To his school. To his class. To his row. She sat right in front of him. She was a regular girl, you know: brownish hair, shirt. But there was one thing about her that was not regular. Not regular at all. She had a thin red ribbon around her neck. Velvet? Maybe.

The kid was like, "Huh. Weird."

The kid thought maybe it had something to do with the French Revolution. In French Revolution times, there were these parties called the Victims' Balls (or whatever that is in French), where the guests would show up in decapitation chic. They had haircuts like the kind that guillotine victims were given. They'd do a dance with jerking head movements like when the guillotine victims got their heads chopped off. And most of all, they wore *red ribbons around their necks*, symbolizing the chop-off that the guillotines did to their victims.

"Big fan of the French Revolution?" the kid asked.

"What? No," said the girl. "They were about to teach about it at my old school, but I moved here, and I guess they already taught about it here, so if I want to learn about it, I'll have to do it on my own, which I bet I'll never get around to."

And she was right. She wasn't the type to fill her extra-curricular hours with learning about history. But she *was* the type to always wear this ribbon *around her neck*! And she was the type, when she was a grown-up adult and the kid was an adult too, to, over the years, have fallen in love with him, which was good news, because he fell in love with her too.

"I love you, you know," said the new girl when she was an adult woman.

"Well, that's fortunate," said the kid, who was now an adult guy, "because I love you too."

Now, it's not like the guy didn't sometimes ask about what the deal was with that ribbon. He asked when they were kids.

"What's the deal with that ribbon?" he said when he was a kid.

"Someday, maybe, I'll tell you," she said, but she may as well have said, "Come on, I'll never actually tell you."

They fell in love many times over the years. They were each other's first kiss and prom dates and breakups and get-back-togethers and break-up-for-goods when they went to different colleges, which, that's how that always goes and also that's how it always should go.

They didn't see each other for years, but when they were each in their hometown for Thanksgiving, the fourth most romantic national holiday, they not only ran into each other, they fell back in love. They were each other's first break-up-for-good-only-not-reallys and they were each other's first in-love-forever-this-time-probablys.

The question arose again about the ribbon, because she always wore it and always had. And on the eve of the rehearsal dinner for their wedding, which, oh yeah, they were getting married to each other (or so they thought), the guy asked again.

"What's the deal with that ribbon?" asked the guy.

"Someday, maybe, I'll tell you," she said again, like she did every time he asked, which was not so often, but not never. Otherwise, they had complete transparency in their relationship. Total trust. They told each other everything. Except one thing.

That night, the guy had a nightmare. In his nightmare, the guy was reading the story "The Tell-Tale Heart" by Edgar Allan Poe, in which the sound of a heartbeat drove the unnamed narrator mad. In the guy's dream, it was a throat-beat. A telltale throat that didn't tell a tale so much as suggested one and kept that tale hidden underneath a ribbon. In the story in the nightmare, the unnamed narrator was so gripped by the mystery of this ribbon that he was overcome by it. He became sweaty and obsessed. The guy woke up before his alarm because of how intensely the nightmare had nightmared him.

He kept thinking about the nightmare all day. He turned it around in his head like some dough you might knead to mix the ingredients and add strength and texture to bread or pasta. When you do this to a memory, you are able to see why it resonates with you in order to "bake" the thoughts into the "bread" of a conclusion or the "pasta" of a practical concern.

The guy *had* to know about the ribbon. Or really wanted to, at least. He did the only thing he felt he *could* do. He asked his fiancée about it.

She could sense from what the guy said and how he said it that he really wanted to know about the ribbon he was asking her about.

Also *she* had had a nightmare. An unnamed narrator who did not respect boundaries pulled the ribbon off from around her neck and then murdered her with a bed, which is what happened in "The Tell-Tale Heart." Edgar Allan Poe's narrator killed an old man with a bed somehow for the offense of having a big weird eye. How did he kill him? Suffocation? Blunt force trauma? The story did not say and the dream did not clarify. Why did the guy and the woman each have "The Tell-Tale Heart" on their mind?

That is a mystery. There are some mysteries that never get solved, but the mystery of the ribbon was not one of those, as you will soon see. . . .

"I can go to a rehearsal dinner without knowing everything about you," the man said. "I can eat the dinner, no problem. And I can eat the dessert, too. You *know* I can eat the dessert, but can I go to a wedding with you, where we get married to each other, without knowing about that ribbon?"

"Of course you can," the woman replied to him. "But you won't have to. Tonight, after the rehearsal dinner, I will remove the ribbon so that you don't have to marry someone who is a fractional mystery to you."

That night, back in the inn— Oh! They were staying at an inn on the property where they were getting married. The inn was hundreds of years old. Dark and terrible things had happened there. Things that would make you shudder in fright or scream in terror, depending on you.

The things that happened there happened in other stories, some in this very volume.

In *this* story, the guy sat in a bed with his fiancée, the woman. The woman lifted two handfuls of fingers to her throat. Ten fingers rose slowly on two hands suspended by two wrists toward the neck of the woman. Toward the ribbon there. The fingers on the hands of the woman slowly untied the ribbon on the neck of her. The guy and the woman had each stopped breathing or blinking or anything. The only thing at all was the small sound of ribbon being pulled off a neck.

And then her head fell off.

Is . . .

what

the

tattoo

underneath the ribbon said.

The guy read the words to himself silently, but moving his lips. She turned, the woman, to look at the guy. What would he think?

Would he think she was a monster, for having delighted in the anticipation of this moment for all the parts of their lives that mattered? He did not. He laughed harder than she knew he could. She laughed too. With him. Because of him.

If it were possible to get even more married than they were going to, that's what they would have done. They were full up of love, and they got as married as anyone ever had, and they stayed that way for the rest of their whole entire natural lives.

THE SAD, SAD STORY OF THE 100% KILLER

The 100% Killer woke up in a hospital. He was banged up and bruised. Sour tempered and sore. He had bandages around his right hand, past his wrist, to his elbow. His left hand was cuffed to the rail of a hospital bed. He was caught.

Not for long, he thought.

"You're up." The police detective sitting at his bedside stood up. "Good. I'm Detective Moon, and you're under arrest."

"How many people are in this hospital?" the 100% Killer asked.

"No, no," said Detective Moon. "Take it easy. Start with

'What happened?' Work your way up to numbers."

But numbers were what the 100% Killer liked. He was a numbers guy. He always had been.

Mathacre! the high school newspaper headline read as it detailed his math team's victory at regionals. *Very high math scores on PSATs and SATs!* the family Christmas letter read as it detailed his parents' pride in his math achievements. *Math scholarship,* the math scholarship paperwork detailed the scholarship in math for which he qualified. "Don't just hold the sign; spin it around," ordered the boss at the shop where the 100% Killer, or Doug, as he was known then, worked.

And so he did, as he worked the summer months as a sign-spinner outside a mobile phone store in a strip mall. Dressed as a stoplight-red phone, spinning a go-light-green sign advertising 100% off. He'd spin the arrow around and around, but he'd always land pointing toward the store's entrance.

Doug was helpful, like most math-minded people are. That is, until he snapped, like only a fraction of math-minded people do.

He snapped for three reasons. Reason one is that it was hot. It was a record-setting summer, heat-wise, and the humidity was also dangerously high, even more so in a phone costume. His brains were too full of math to handle being twice-baked between sun and suit. The second reason he snapped is that customers are rude. Some of them tried to dial him. That never didn't hurt.

The third reason, and this might be the biggest reason, is there was a demon whispering evil commands into his brain.

You see, the store was next to a hobby shop that sold games, models, and figurines. Hobbyists congregated there every weekend to paint or construct projects together. This is where a pair of twins with a mildly haunted, majorly termite-chewed ventriloquist dummy found a hobbyist interested in restoring the dummy to its original condition.

Mosmogon, the demon in the dummy, was also interested in this restoration. With the last of the termites that had nearly consumed him now providing his sustenance, he bided his time. He tasted the mindscapes of those who came through the hobby shop. All such kind people. None with switches the demon could flip. He reached out the tongue of his mind farther and farther until he found Doug. He could taste Doug's frustration, love of math, and capacity for evil.

Mosmogon gained strength by eroding Doug's.

"One hundred percent," he brain-whispered again and again. "Kill one hundred percent of them."

Mosmogon's mental tongue licked away at the lollipop of Doug's humanity.

On one particularly hot and customer-dense day, Doug disappeared, and the 100% Killer surfaced. The 100% Killer bought an X-Acto knife from the hobby shop. He sharpened Doug's green arrow as sharp as he could make it. The 100% Killer followed Doug's arrow into the phone store to baptize the 100% arrow in blood and make it his own. Unfortunately, the arrow wasn't deadly, no matter how sharp. Fortunately for the 100% Killer, and unfortunately for everyone in the shop, he still had that X-Acto blade.

News reports told of the Cell Phone Killer because security cameras showed him doing his grisly business in that promotional suit. *That will not do,* he thought. From then on, he focused on what was important: comfortable clothes and his urge to kill EVERYONE—100% of any group he started killing. The 100% Killer limited his sprees to small, manageable locations. Minimal crowds. Low population. Antique stores. Cafés. Bed-and-breakfasts.

The 100% Killer had most recently murdered everyone staying in a small inn on an estate they used for events. It was lovely. He really liked killing there. The air was undistilled springtime. Until he distilled it with the screams of his victims. Even still, between the landscape and the fireflies, it was picturesque.

"What happened to you is . . ." Detective Moon stood

now and looked at the 100% Killer's chart. "You were flee-
ing the scene, and you must have heard the sirens. See,
you left someone alive at that inn, and she called us."

The 100% Killer sneered at the detective. He wouldn't
have left anyone alive.

She's just trying to make me angry, the 100% Killer
thought. *I'll make her angry right back when I kill one hundred percent of her.*

"Lovely inn, by the way. Before you got there, anyway. You sped off on those winding country roads.
Faster than you wanted, I bet, because of the sirens, I
bet. Sloppy. You took a tumble off the road. Fortunately
for you, you wound up in one piece. It just wasn't a complete piece."

Detective Moon held up the chart for the 100% Killer
to read but realized the font size was going to be too small
for that to work. She pointed instead at the 100% Killer's
right hand. She made a little swirly gesture to indicate
the bandages around it. "You're down a hand."

The 100% Killer looked at his bandages. There was a
hand underneath.

"Well, you *were.* There was some confusion, and by the
time we got it all sorted out, well, you're the lucky recipi-
ent of a transplant. As far as parts are concerned, you're
back up to one hundred percent."

The 100% Killer scowled like killers and teenagers do.

"Once they say it's okay to move you, I'll ride you over to processing, and we can start the rest of your incarcerated life directly."

The detective slumped back in her chair. Her stomach growled. She was more worried about lunch than she was about the dangerous man in the hospital bed.

Her mistake, thought the 100% Killer, then *he* growled. "How many people are in this hospital?"

"Back to that, are we?"

"I never left it," the 100% Killer said. "Just like you'll never leave here."

The 100% Killer sat up suddenly, pulling his left arm with all his might, using the chain of the handcuff to separate the metal arm of the bed from the rest. He threw the metal bar into his new right hand to break it in, give it its first kill—this detective, who refused to tell him how much work he had ahead. Someone would tell him eventually. But first, the detective must die.

Only . . .

His right hand held the metal bar in the air, straining against his arm. It wouldn't swing.

"Come on!" he yelled at his hand, to no avail.

The 100% Killer was outraged. Detective Moon was on her feet, reaching for her gun. The 100% Killer charged Detective Moon, knocking her down as he raced out of the room and into the next. An old man lay in a bed, looking terrified. The 100% Killer raised the bar again. Once more he couldn't bring it down.

"Wake up!" The murderer yelled to his disobedient appendage. "Get to work!"

Room after room, the 100% Killer tried his hand at his craft only to be thwarted again and again. He started this hospital swath at 0%, and he wasn't getting any better.

"What's wrong with me?" he bellowed.

"I can answer that," a doctor said coolly. "I'm Dr. Senstrand. I performed your surgery today. I heard what you're going through. I checked it out. It turns out that your hand donor was a pacifist. He'd never hurt a fly. That's the kind of hand you have now."

If a hand could remember a life before, this hand would have had images of picking flowers, painting sunsets, and lighting candles. It would have heard acoustic guitar music and seagulls at the oceanside. Textures and touches would ring warmly in the hand's memory. Manicures and lotion.

Care and respect. The hand had been well loved and had loved well in return.

"A non-murderer's hand?" the 100% Killer cried. "Noooooo!"

He dropped to his knees. The bar fell and rolled noisily away from him. Uniformed officers rushed around Dr. Senstrand, grabbed the 100% Killer and handcuffed him to another bed, but they needn't have.

The 100% Killer would never kill again.

THE MOST DANGEROUS GAME

Part 1

A t Camp Moosejaw, there were some campers who cheered for the kind of rainy afternoon where outdoor activities would be canceled. The kids in the Finches cabin had been waiting the whole sunny summer session for a dreary day like this. It was time for the Park twins to break the All-Game from out of their steamer trunk and combine it with the games in the camp's game nook to create this year's All-Game: Summer Edition.

The Parks were stuck on a rainy canoe trip campout down on the far end of Lake Tarleton.

Their bunkmates Mauricio and Rainier had the most

experience with the All-Game: Summer Edition. They stepped up to lead the game.

Rainier dealt out cards—some standard playing cards, some from various card-based role-playing games, some cards from board games, and some tarot cards thrown in for what Firetruck called "spice" and DD called "tempting fate."

Rainier passed out pouches of letter tiles from a few different word-making games and doled out dice—ten six-sided, six ten-sided, three twenty-sided, and a pop-o-matic for every player. He distributed a murder weapon from the murder game or a player token from the capitalism game that except for the thimble (too small), top hat (a hat), and battleship (too big) could be used as a murder weapon.

While Rainier saw to the players, Mauricio laid down the boards. Fortunately, the cabins at Moosejaw were big enough to contain a full-sized picnic table because the All-Game: Summer Edition took up a ton of space. Firetruck's prized Ouija board went down first, underneath everything, because of course it did. A couple of rooms of a haunted-house game went over the Ouija board again, of course. Every time the All-Game was played, it built upon this perfectly hauntable foundation.

Next, Mauricio layered some train tracks from a mass transit game and a card with a strip of highway from a car-racing card game. Each of the other players picked a board from the game pile and placed it around the center board to create the entire field of the first heat. Game play would start in the middle and travel out in a spiral until the players reached the edges. Every board had pieces of other games picked at random and scattered around, with more to be layered on top in the second heat.

They were almost ready to begin.

The players then got to vote whether they started in a bustling hub in a cross-country train journey or else they could commence from a starting line in shiny open-wheel single-seater racing cars. The latter choice had an added difficulty of being from a mid-twentieth-century game that was entirely in French.

The other players from the Finches were each named John but went by Hank, Nat, and Killian. Almost no John at Moosejaw went by John. Original John (the camp's first John), Super John (the camp's best John), and Kaiju John (who was not a city-stomping giant reptile, but not for lack of trying) were as close as you got. Vi from the Sparrows was also playing. She and Nat were BFFFFs. Only they knew what the extra *F*s stood for. Vi lived for the All-Game: Summer Edition. She played it the most out of any camper at Moosejaw. A few summers back, when she was only nine, she came the closest to winning that anyone ever has.

To win, you cross heat after heat of multigame play-scapes until you get to a magical city where you must defeat the evil prince, which means defeating the witch, which also means defeating her friend.

"The witch's friend is most formidable, indeed," Mauricio explained to new players and refreshed for returning players. Rainier doled out player pieces and various disks, gems, and tokens by color. Hank was blue, Nat was black, Killian was red, Vi was green, Rainier was white, and Mauricio was orange.

The players rolled and popped all of their dice to see who started. As soon as it was decided that Nat was first, the very moment the All-Game: Summer Edition actually began, that's when it happened. . . .

The cabin flickered, whirled, and faded around the players until it disappeared. A train station surrounded them now. It was so barely lit as to nearly seem like it was in black and white.

Only one thing was for certain anymore. Rainier and Mauricio were no longer running the game.

Part 2

The Park siblings lived for summer camp. The night got a different kind of dark in the woods than at home.

Campfires were the Parks' kind of spooky. Tales of masked killers and lake creatures abounded. Also, there were s'mores. This summer, their favorite cousin, Emerson, was joining them at Camp Moosejaw.

They went shopping for a gift to bring her. They went to the pawn shop because it was like a permanent garage sale. It was located in the same strip mall as the hobby shop where they had left their dummy to get restored. It was on the other side of the cell phone store where everyone got murdered. The Park kids had discovered the pawn shop when they went to the phone store to see if they could meet a ghost. A tall adult told DD and Firetruck they had just missed all of them.

When the Park twins found out that the locket had been sold to the pawn shop because it had been full of spiders, they had to have it. They decided it was the perfect gift for Emerson, as long as they never told her about the spiders.

When the demon Mosmogon found out that the locket had been full of spiders, he moved in immediately. Mosmogon had helped invent spiders, after all. The locket was silver, so when the demon settled in, he was stuck again. Silver inhibits demons, which is why demons rarely inhabit silver. Never on purpose. Never by design. If he had known it was silver, he never would have transferred his essence inside, but he was only strong enough for the jump from the dummy into the locket, thanks to his successful efforts corrupting an arrow-spinner. The demon had not been capable of discerning the locket's material composition. Not with just one arrow-spinner under his belt. He could sense, however, that his prison had once again been purchased by the same children who longed so much for his presence. He yearned to grant them their wish. To make them regret it.

The Park siblings bought the spider locket for Emerson. Once again, they had a demonic possession, and once again, they never knew it. They made each other promise to remember not to call it "the spider locket" in front of Emerson. They packed it in their steamer trunk along with the supplies listed on the Camp Moosejaw supply checklist and as much of the All-Game as they could fit.

At the end of any airplane flight, there is an announcement to be careful retrieving bags from the overhead bins as items may have shifted during the journey. The same bumpy redistribution happens to checked baggage too big to be in the overhead bin—a steamer trunk, say, that has been jostled by the same journey. When that baggage contains a demon in a locket formerly containing spiders, be extra careful, as the clasp on that locket may have been knocked open by the corner of a deck of cards and released an old evil into some slightly used and willfully, utterly mismatched sets of tabletop games.

Part 3

The released demon had released the All-Game: Summer Edition into the world. Now it was the players who were trapped, the game manifesting around them.

"Like that one movie," said Hank. "And its sequel. That's what this is like."

"No, this is more like the movie that the movie you mean is a remake of," said Killian, "and its sequel."

"It's like every story about people playing role-playing games," said Rainier, who had read a lot of that type of story.

"They get sucked into them," agreed Mauricio, who had written a few of that type of story.

"I notice we're still us," Nat said. "We're just carrying our letter tile pouches, a pocket full of dice, and our murder weapons, which have become real." He pointed to the Boston terrier from the capitalism game that had come to life in Hank's arms. "We're just us, with some stuff, wearing the colors we chose for our player pieces." He pointed to his black shirt and pants. "That feels like a missed opportunity. We could have been adults, or at least teenagers. Heroes of some kind."

"I hear when the Parks play this at home, they use action figures for the pieces," Vi told them. "It'd be cool to be a robot that turns into a car."

"I'd be a space knight," said Nat.

"I think if we were space knights or robots or super-heroes, that'd make it even more like the movie like this," said Hank. "Or its sequel."

"Yeah," agreed Killian. "Or the originals."

"But between those and the RPG stories Rainier mentioned, I feel like we can safely say this situation is not copycatting any particular one," Nat said.

They all agreed that their situation felt more or less original.

"Plus, unlike those other ones, it looks like there's a demon or something responsible for this one we're in," Vi added.

"What do you mean?" asked Mauricio.

"Well for one thing—the train game is colorful and bright. This train station is dreary and decrepit. Every-thing is colorless and spooky. It feels like midnight. And then there's that," she said, pointing up at the sky, where the moonlit clouds took the shape of the face of the demon Mosmogon looking down at them.

On being noticed, the clouds dispersed as if that was what they were going to do anyway. The clouds all but whistled innocently as they scattered. The Boston terrier barked at a nearby patch of darkness.

"What's going on?" Alex, the Finches counselor, asked, appearing out of nowhere alongside Stef, the waterfront counselor. "What is this?"

"It's the All-Game: Summer Edition," Mauricio said. "We were playing it. Now we're in it."

Alex looked around, at the moon, the horizon, the train station, as if he were trying to figure out exactly which element in particular baffled him most among the abundance of incongruity.

"It . . . ," he started, but trailed off as he took another whole entire look at everything. "It doesn't look like summer."

Stef let out a laugh, but not the kind that happens when something is funny. It was the kind of laugh that happens when there's nothing else to do. The kind with a little tear in it.

"What are you guys doing in here?" Vi asked. "You're not playing the game that sucked us inside."

"We got caught in the rain at the waterfront," Alex said as a sound reminiscent of remote-control airplanes started in the distance. "It stopped raining for a minute, and we ran back to the cabin before it started again." The sound was getting closer. "We came in, and then here we were. Just entering the cabin gets you in the game. This *is*

original." The sound was so close now.

It was here.

Six sleek Formula 1 race cars pulled up in front of them, idling dangerously, looking like brightly polished kazoos on wheels. Six drivers got out. Skeletons in crash helmets and twill racing jackets, white or powder blue with navy and orange racing stripes from the 1960s, when the cars and game were made, and perhaps when these drivers would have been alive. "Skeletons," Alex said. "I know this game. I donated it. There aren't skeletons in this game!"

"*Zut alors!*" one of the skeletons said, pointing past the campers.

Behind the kids stood a wiry man in a rectangular mask and blue-gray coveralls. On his chest, on his T-shirt, where the coveralls didn't cover, were the words that struck fear in every camper at Moosejaw: TARLETON JACK!

The killer grunted and looked from the campers to the counselors, like a shopper in a grocery store deciding between apples. Tarleton Jack was choosing a victim.

"He must have come in the cabin to kill us!" Vi hissed. "And now he means to do it here!"

Tarleton Jack raised a tire iron to do the kind of violence with the tool for which it was not intended. Before he got the chance to completely shatter Alex's skull, however, Tarleton Jack got hit by a ghost train.

"Un train fantôme," said a skeleton.

"Un boo choo-choo," agreed another.

Part 4

Mauricio and Rainier had gobbled up campfire stories of Tarleton Jack since their first year at camp. They had talked into the wee hours about what they would do if he made his way to Moosejaw one day. Where they would hide. How they would escape him. How they would get away. What they would use for booby traps.

To see him in person froze them in terror and delight. To see him be dispatched by the semi-corporeal spirit of a locomotive in a demon's realization of the All-Game:

Summer Edition was nearly too much for them to wrap their heads around.

Vi was having her own issue dealing with the idea that if the game had not enveloped them, a masked murderer would have just walked into the cabin, and how would that have gone for them? She was shaken.

Hank was also not happy about the murderer. "I knew from the second I heard about Tarleton Jack getting revenge on the math camp across the lake for not killing him, that someday he would come for revenge on me for also not killing him."

"What are you talking about?" asked Killian. "He didn't kill everyone at the math camp across the lake. He killed everyone at the equestrian camp across the lake and down."

"No," said Hank, looking worriedly at where Tarleton Jack had stood, as the ghostly caboose of a phantasmagoric locomotive disappeared in the distance. "He killed everyone at the math camp. Every counselor and camper. Some with their own protractors."

"He killed everyone at the equestrian camp because they ran over him with their horses but didn't kill him. And thus began his sort-of revenge," said Killian. "What do you think they ran over him with at the math camp? A ruler?"

"A car," said Hank. "A counselor's car is what I heard."

"The 100% Killer killed everyone at the math camp," said Killian. "That's what I heard. He used to go there. Couldn't solve a problem and it drove him to seek his revenge. Turns out the answer was one hundred percent. Killing one hundred percent. Of people. At a place. What do you think, Nat?"

"Huh?" asked Nat, who was too busy digging in his tile pouch to have followed the conversation. "He's up." Nat nodded toward where Tarleton Jack had been thrown by the train.

Tarleton Jack was standing, once again inconvenienced but not killed by vehicular collision. The visor was open. He closed the visor and straightened the mask. He pulled his coveralls closed, but they were torn, revealing more of his T-shirt. TARLETON JACK, it said, AND TOW, it continued.

"Tarleton Jack and Tow? What is that? A garage?" asked Stef.

"Yeah, I took my car there once," said Alex. "He must have worked there. No wonder he carries a tire iron. No wonder he wears a welding mask. His name's not Tarleton Jack at all. Look. It's Bill." Alex pointed at a patch that said BILL.

"This feels weird to know," said Hank.

"I'm still going to call him Tarleton Jack," said Killian.

"When you talk to him?" asked Hank.

"No. Like, in my head. When I'm running away from him. Which, let's do that now."

Tarleton Jack had started lumbering toward them. He stopped, though, got down on the ground, lifted the visor on his mask, and groped in the mist. He came up again, now holding his tire iron. He gave it a twirl like a marching band leader's baton and lumbered toward them once more.

And then primal sounds rose. Ground-shaking sounds that froze everyone.

"*L'hippopotame,*" said a skeleton.

"*L'hippopotame,*" said another.

"*L'hippopotame.*" The rest nodded.

"L'what?" asked Rainier.

"Hippopotamus," Vi answered gravely. "The world's most dangerous land animal. There are four of them," she said, having laid down their game in the direction the sound came from. "And they're hungry."

The hippos bellowed once more, and the sound was otherworldly. Vi looked up at the clouds. The demon's face was back. It was smiling.

"I bet they're worse than ordinary hippos. Don't look up, but the demon is back and he's messing with everything. Making it supernaturally worse. Skeletons. Ghost train." She noticed Nat was doing something. "What are you doing, Nat?"

"Trying my luck," Nat said as he threw letters back into the pouch. He put together the letters in his hand: S-W-O-R-D. With the sound of lightning and metal, the tiles turned into a sword. "Well, there you go." He grinned.

Nat was that type. A mix of crafty and lucky. His nickname, Nat, was short for "Nat 20," as in the natural 20, the best roll you can get on a twenty-sided die in a role-playing game. Nat rolled so many nat 20s, he got a nickname. If he were rolling now, that's what he would have gotten, having put together a sword like this. He used it to dispatch a skeleton.

"Sacrebleu!" its skull said in the air as its body collapsed.

Nat jumped into the skeleton's car and revved the engine.

"Spell some weapons, waste some skeletons, let's get out of here before *les hippopotames* get here. But first—" Nat gunned his car and ran over Tarleton Jack.

"Come on. The only way out in one of the movies this is like is through. Let's go defeat a prince, a witch, and her friend!"

What followed promised to be a harrowing trip through monsterfied demonic multigame playscapes with an unrelated relentless masked killer at their heels.

The Parks' dream come true.

The Parks, however, never got to see a second of it.

All they knew was what everyone at Camp Moosejaw knew. That on the night of the storm, six campers and two counselors disappeared and were never seen again.

Well, the Parks knew one more thing than that. That the All-Game: Summer Edition had also disappeared. They sensed that the two were related. They hoped to solve it next summer, but summer camps don't get to lose six campers and two counselors and then stay open the next summer.

Two summers later was a whole other terrible story.

VAMPIRES AREN'T LIARS!

Vampires are straight shooters!

Justin the editor from the book company is here!

He's here in the house!

Despite my doubts, Evan called Justin the editor after all. It took a while for Justin the editor to get here because Evan didn't use a phone. He haunted Justin the editor's dreams!

These vampires! They have a particular way of doing things. Evan haunted Justin the editor's dreams and compelled him to come! Then why was Evan avoiding me? I guess maybe he wasn't! What matters is that Justin the editor is here!

Hoosh! That's what it sounds like in my ears right now. I'm so excited. I really have to hand it to these vampires. So encouraging. I'm feeling so confident for tonight when I tell my story—maybe I'll tell a few. I'm confident because I've been telling story after story. Getting good feedback from the Baker's Coven. That's what the vampires call themselves, by the way.

Oh, I should tell you a little about them, in case it's helpful.

They call themselves the Baker's Coven because there are thirteen of them. That's a lot to keep track of.

There's Evan—he's in charge of the group. He's really friendly, like a substitute teacher who has you call him by his first name.

Kitty—she's in charge of Evan. She's tall, thin, and absolutely dramatic. I have seen her react to things with her whole entire body—lifting her arms over her head and rearing back laughing or moaning. Every time she does it, she reminds me of the blowy man that bobs and bounces in front of the supermarket.

Then there are, like, eleven more vampires who just go by Count. They're great too. Well dressed. Honestly, I think they coordinate outfits with each other. They were the ones who watched me eat, but they stopped doing that. They come out for the stories and house meetings and then they keep to themselves the rest of the time. When they come out, they greet each other by title. So it's like one of them will come say hello to Evan and Kitty, who each say hello back by title. So it goes . . .

"Evan. Kitty," a count will say.

"Count," Evan will say back.

"Count," Kitty will say.

Then another comes out and it's . . .

"Count. Evan. Kitty."

"Count," Evan will say.

Then "Count," Kitty says.

"Count," the other count says.

Then a few more will emerge, and soon everyone's saying . . .

"Count."

"Count." "Count." "Count."

"Count."

"Count." "Count." "Count." "Count." "Count."

"Count."

And on and on and on. It sounds like a roomful of people saying the word "count" willy-nilly, but when everyone is greeted, they just stop.

Their watercolors aren't so bad. I mean, they're terrible, but they're earnest. The counts aren't claiming they're making masterpieces. They have all the time in the world. So what if they fill some of it up with mediocre kindergarten-level art projects? If that brings them joy, guess what: they deserve joy. Maybe they just started.

I should encourage them in their creative pursuit. They sure encouraged me in mine. And they brought Justin the editor!

Maybe if you're reading this, the vampires are right now helping your dreams come true. If so, please reach out and let me know how it's going, what your dreams are. We should stay in touch, friend; we, the beneficiaries of vampiric generosity. Or get in touch, I guess. And then stay there. I feel a kinship with you. You know that. I always have.

ANOTHER STORY IN THIS VERY VOLUME

The tall exorcist drove his small car to a quaint inn.

"Quaint" often means "watch your head." To the tall exorcist, it always did.

The tall exorcist had bumped his head in quaint cottages, quaint inns like this one, quaint restaurants, a quaint bookshop, even a quaint grocery store once in the Pacific Northwest.

The tall exorcist lowered his head to enter the lovely surroundings. He folded himself behind the lobby desk, a space that would have been perfect for a shorter exorcist.

"May I have your attention?" the tall exorcist asked.

Wisps of energy, the ghosts of the recently dead,

congregated at the sound of the tall man's voice, forming features as they arrived in the lobby.

"Thank you. Good news, bad news, then more good news. Good news, your murderer has been caught. Bad news, you"—he gave the wisps a look of sincere sympathy—"have been murdered. My condolences."

A concerned ghost coalesced a hand and raised it.

"If you wouldn't mind saving questions until the end, I hope to answer them all."

The ghost lowered his hand.

"The last bit of good news I mentioned is that I'm here to help you," the tall exorcist continued. "Now, what a ghost—and you're all ghosts—needs to do to move on is to complete a task they hadn't gotten to complete in life. None of you got the chance to check out of the hotel," he told them. "All you have to do is line up. Tell me your room number and that you'd like to check out and that'll do it. Exit the lobby and go into the circle of pure light right outside."

The tall exorcist looked at the concerned ghost to see if he still had a question. He did not.

A good two-thirds of the ghosts did as they were directed. A few of them had forgotten their room number. The Tall Exorcist assured them it was fine, because it was. They completed their leftover task and took the circle of light to wherever they were supposed to go.

That left about one third of them. Indignant, resistant ghosts who would rather throw furniture at the tall exorcist than listen to him.

"Why should we believe you?" one of them asked.

"I am angry," another declared in the kind of voice you use right before you throw furniture.

The tall exorcist knew that he only had the day to get these ghosts on their way, lest they become poltergeists. Poltergeists are spirits who forget who they were in favor of how they feel. They feel angry. They walk the line between throwing temper tantrums and being temper tantrums.

The day went on like any long day in customer service. The tall exorcist stood patiently and cramped behind the desk. He heard every unsatisfied customer's complaints about the inn and life. Their stay at both had been cut short.

"I'm sorry to hear that," he said. "I'd love to get you out of here and on your way."

He tolerated their venting at him as if it were his fault, which it was not, and then asked again if they would check out and move on.

The tall exorcist had a hard time understanding why anyone wouldn't go to the circle of light, once the situation was explained to them. He knew that regular people weren't walking around keeping track of the latest details of what to do when you're a ghost. That's why he was here. To explain without judgment. He brought out the latest research in the field and laid it on the desk for all to read. He offered to answer any question as best as he could.

His calm tone did him no favors.

"We find it patronizing," he was told.

Facts and information did no good either.

"We are intellectually incurious," they said, preferring to intuit facts from feelings than to read the current thinking from the finest minds in the field.

"Expertise is condescending to people who don't have it, and I'm people who don't have it," one of them said.

"My gut says to throw a fit," a ghost said. "And a chair," he added.

Elegant chairs scraped against the pristine hardwood floor as they moved back from the tasteful coffee tables.

"There's no need for that," said the tall exorcist, who liked these chairs.

The scraping squeaking chairs circled the room like lions.

"All right. If you're not going to listen to reason—" the tall exorcist began, but he was interrupted.

"Whose reason?" a belligerent ghost shouted. "Your reason?"

"Who are you?" a bellicose ghost yelled. "What are your leanings?"

"Do you have ulterior motives?" They were riling each other up.

"You aren't like me," a hostile ghost rumbled, "so I don't trust you."

"Me neither," one said, then another, then another.

This is getting bad, thought the tall exorcist.

The tasteful chairs lifted into the air and circled faster, like speedy flying lions.

The tall exorcist assessed two impending dangers: he could be hurt, or the chairs could. The tall exorcist always tried his best to prevent unnecessary damage to both furniture and self.

The tall exorcist resigned himself to a solution that might prevent such harm.

"Now, I'm not supposed to show you this," he said, which commanded the ghosts' attention. "This is definitely not for you."

The chairs hovered in place as if they were lions who were also interested in what the tall exorcist was about to show them.

The tall exorcist opened the closet door behind the desk.

Inside was a lazily rotating dark blue vortex that sometimes shrieked.

"What's that?" asked the belligerent ghost.

"I bet it's the real light," said the bellicose ghost about the swirling dark circle.

"All I know is that none of you are supposed to go in there," said the tall exorcist. "You're supposed to go toward the light outside."

The chairs collected, stacking themselves on the desk, nearly touching the quaint ceiling. The tall exorcist judged the stack. The chairs wouldn't scuff the desk if they were taken down carefully.

One by one, the angry ghosts went spitefully into the dark vortex.

The tall exorcist protested insincerely: "Please don't" and "You're going to get me in such trouble" and "Oh no, you are teaching me a real lesson."

With the last of them gone, he closed the closet door. He didn't know exactly where the dark vortex led, nor did he care to ever find out. It was, he was fairly certain, not ideal. He knew for absolute sure that it was full of terrible company.

The tall exorcist made sure the inn was empty before carefully taking some truly well-crafted chairs down off the desk.

MORE IN STORE

R J was out, just driving around. He hadn't done it in a while. He used to like to just go where the roads took him, and then he didn't anymore. Tonight, they took him to old Foxhound Road. And there, in his headlights, was the hitchhiker. They weren't the same headlights, it wasn't the same car, but there was no mistaking it: it was the same hitchhiker. She held out her thumb. He nodded and unlocked the door.

She got in. She sat. She smiled, relieved. She somehow knew he'd come. She felt and fought the urge to hug him. She wanted to tell him so many things, as if she'd ever spoken to him before. She had to remember that she hadn't.

She held up her hand and pointed.

"Finger-gun style," said RJ. "That's different."

He drove where she indicated, pointing with her pointer finger.

"I don't really know why I came down here," said RJ. "I think I hoped to go to that corner and not see you and think that whatever you were, you were done. Gone now. Moved on. At peace. Somewhere warm."

This is what she remembered about him. He was sweet.

"I'm sorry," she said.

His eyes went wide.

"Your voice is the same as I imagined it," he said.

"Can we just pull over for a little?" she asked.

"Let's go up here. We're right by the lake."

They parked by the lake. The moon had done the same.

Outside, was another crisp night. Only RJ felt it.

Meg looked out over the lake. RJ looked at Meg.

"You're a little see-through," RJ said. "You weren't last time."

Something else struck him. *What was it?*

He realized what it was, and it took his breath away.

"You sparkle."

Meg felt the urge to reach for him. To touch him. Just put her hand on his. As a phantom, she was mostly intangible. She had touched some doors and plenty of coats, but never a person. She hadn't thought she should. She wasn't sure if she could.

"That sparkle is the moon reflecting off the lake. You can see it through me." She liked that he thought it was her.

"Oh. Still. Cool."

No kind of foreshadowing happened here.

He got a little chilly, so they got back in the car.

She told him about the first jacket that she stole, as punishment for a lackluster date with a lackluster guy. His name was Travis. He had baby-duck blond hair and a keen interest in talking about himself. "When he came back to get his jacket the next day, my mom told him I'd moved away but had had such a good time on our date that I brought his coat with me to remember him by."

The used-coat store idea had started as a joke, but she and her mother egged each other on and, once they landed on the phantom hitchhiker ruse, they started raking in the coats, and it turned serious.

RJ was shocked to learn that she had been alive when they met. He was horrified that she'd died since.

As they talked, she was guiding him along down this road, over to that other one. Left at the light.

RJ told her about how he thought he had it all figured out at nineteen, how college then traveling abroad disabused him of that idea. He realized then that his brush with Meg had planted the seed of what he had come to believe, which is that in a world with phantom hitchhikers in it, there was more in the universe than he could know at nineteen or ever, so he'd best stay open to it all.

It truly warmed Meg to hear that she hadn't just been a thing that went bump in his past.

They got where they were going. The used-coat store.

RJ realized how often he'd passed this place without ever noticing it, even though that was his coat up there in the window display.

Meg opened the door for RJ. From behind the counter, Meg's mother waved hello and mouthed, *Sorry.* RJ mouthed, *It's okay.*

"I believe that one belongs to you." Meg offered RJ his old coat back.

"No thank you," he said. "I'm not that person anymore."

"You're a little bit still that person," Meg said.

"On the inside, sure," he agreed. "But not where coats go."

"Well, pick any coat you like. On the house." She smiled. "Unless it's too expensive, then it's half off."

"It's not necessary," he said. "I have a coat. I'm just happy to see you again. Is that ridiculous?"

"I need you to pick a coat. When I died, I got back all the inventory we'd stolen. I've been returning them one by one. Paid what I owe. I saved you for— You're my last."

"Last," he said, gesturing at all the coats. "What about all these coats?"

"Those were obtained ethically," Meg explained.

"If I choose a coat, will you move on?" RJ asked. "Join the great beyond? Find your ultimate reward?"

"I hope not. I don't want to leave my mom all alone in this store forever."

"Don't worry about me, dear," her mom said. "Not ever again. This store was fun, but I think it's time for something new."

"What kind of something new?" Meg asked.

"Maybe it's time I join the great beyond or find my ultimate reward," she said. "You see, I've been dead the whole time."

"What?"

"That's right. Mommy loves a twist ending. I love you. See you when I see you."

She dissipated into bits of stardust, and then she was gone.

"Wow," said Meg. "That was a left turn!"

"It really came out of nowhere," said RJ. "Did you have any idea?"

"No," said Meg, rewinding her thoughts and realizing that some memories made more sense now. Mostly memories of waiters in restaurants ignoring Meg and her mother.

RJ ran his hand through the last of the stardust.

"I don't want you to go," he said. "I want to get to know you more. Oh, man, is that super selfish?"

"It's sweet." She smiled. "Tell you what, let's hang out. Tonight. All night. I want to know you more too. Then at dawn, you pick a coat, and if I disappear and become one with the great beyond, at least we had tonight. What do you think?"

"I'll tell you what," he said." All I know for sure is that there's more in the universe than I could ever know for sure, so I'd best stay open to it."

He held out his hand for her.

"I don't know if I can do that," she said.

"Stay open to it," he smiled.

And she did.

BEST FRIENDS
FOREVER

The alive boy and the ghost boy climbed the tallest tree on the property.

"We're high up, Timothy," said Mikey, the alive boy, trying not to sound as worried as he was.

"Too high?" Timothy, the ghost of a boy, asked.

"Maybe." Mikey had never climbed a tree this tall before.

"Do you want to climb down?" asked Timothy, who had climbed this tree tens of times when he was alive and thousands of times after. "Go work on the fort?"

"Mikey!" Mikey's mom called. "Where are you?"

"Your mom is calling you," Timothy reported, in case

ghost ears worked better than the ears of the flesh.

"I heard her," Mikey said. "Help me get down."

"Do you think your mom would be able to see me? Some people can. Some people can't."

"I don't know." Mikey was starting to panic now. "Help me, please."

"Okay, but I don't know how to help, really." Timothy floated over to Mikey.

"You just have to climb down the way you climbed up except the other way. Toward the ground."

Mikey felt like he was going to fall every time he reached a foot down to find a branch. It was taking forever.

"Maybe I should get your mom, bring her here, and she can help you get down. I'd hate to scare her, though. I'd hate to scare any mom again."

"Just hold on to me to keep me from falling. Like, push me against the tree."

"I can try to do that," Timothy said, "but don't lean back against me for support."

"Why not?" asked Mikey, trying to figure out how not to do that.

"You'll go right through."

Which is exactly what happened.

Mikey was right to be scared. The first sturdy branch he hit on the way down knocked the ghost right out of him. His body rolled off and kept falling all the way to the ground.

"Oh no!" Timothy exclaimed.

"Oh no!" Mikey's ghost yelped.

"That's you!"

"That's me down there!"

"Oh no!"

Mikey's mom called him again.

"I'm gonna be in so much trouble!" Mikey said, scrambling for an idea of what to do. "Go down there," he told Timothy, "and get in my body."

"What?"

"Like when we were playing with those puppets and you squeezed into that marionette to make him dance. Make me stand up. Talk to my mom. Don't let her know I'm . . ." He trailed off the way you do when you're only just dead and don't want to say the word yet because maybe there's a way out of it as long as you don't let your mom know.

"You get down there," countered Timothy, "and you get in your own body and stay there. Go to the hospital. Maybe they can fix it, keep you in it."

"Is that how it works?"

"Definitely not if you stay up there!"

"I'm coming down." Mikey dangled his foot again to reach for a lower branch.

"You need to *hurry*."

"Shhh."

"You can just drop."

"I can't."

"Believe me, you really can."

"Shh. I have to do it this way." Mikey tap-tap-tapped the branch below him.

"Nothing can hurt you now. Just let yourself fall."

"Okay. Yes. Right. Okay. I'm doing it. Letting myself fall. I'm letting go."

He stayed right where he was.

"I'm doing it," Mikey said.

"Do you think you are?" Timothy asked. "Because you're not."

"I'm trying."

"Maybe, but it is not working."

"Shh. I have to do it this way," Mikey said, dangling a foot. "You go in. Marionette me. Fool my mom until I get down there, and I'll go inside my body and go to the hospital in it."

"Fine."

Timothy pushed back from the tree and dropped slowly toward Mikey's body. Timothy steered himself as he drifted and turned himself around so as to be in Mikey's exact position. He landed perfectly in Mikey.

"Nice," said Mikey.

Timothy stood his friend's body up.

"This is hard," Timothy said. "Is it on right? It's like I

have to hold on with all of my—I don't know what to call it. It's like I'm clenching my entire body to keep this on. This is not easy. Hurry up."

Hold on to the body. Hold on, hold on, hold on, Timothy thought to himself.

Mikey dropped to the next branch down. "This is weird. I feel like I should go back up."

"To the branch you died on? That makes sense. It took me forever to get out of my bed when I passed, and by the time I did it, it took a ton of effort, and my mom . . . Everything had moved on."

Mikey's body started to slip off of Timothy. "Whoops!" Timothy said, and he pulled it back up straight.

"Don't talk to me," said Mikey. "Concentrate."

Hold on. Hold on. Hold on. Timothy concentrated.

"Here you are," said Mikey's mom, relieved. "Didn't you hear me calling you?"

Hold on to the body. Answer the question. What does Mikey sound like?

"Yes, I heard." Timothy did his best impression of Mikey's voice.

"I don't sound like that!" Mikey yelled, then clapped his hand over his mouth.

His mother hadn't heard him.

She can't hear Mikey. She can't see him. Hold on to the body. Be more Mikey; keep talking. Hold on, hold on, hold on.

"I was just climbing this tree." He tried to sound more like Mikey. "And I heard you calling, so I climbed down. I was just about to come to you, and here you are."

I'm talking to a mom! Maybe I should hug her. Should I hug her? I want to hug a mom again. Ut! Hold on to the body. Don't hug. Hold on!

Mikey's mother gave "Mikey" a long stare as if he was a book a few inches too far away to be readable, but rather than move the book closer, she was determined to make out the letters.

"Breathe and blink!" Mikey called. "You're not breathing or blinking. Alive people breathe and blink."

He had forgotten to do breathing. He tried to remember which came first? Inhale? Exhale? He decided to start with inhaling. He had forgotten blinking as well. That was easier because blinking is like riding a bike.

Blink. Inhale, exhale, hold on to the body, inhale, exhale, hold on to the body. Blink.

It worked!

Mikey's mother stopped reading her pretend faraway book and shook her head.

"When I was about your age," she said, "my sister and I climbed a tree like this one. Not this tall, kiddo. You're braver than I was."

Timothy smiled Mikey's mouth. He liked Mikey's mom already.

"I fell," she said. "Broke my arm. Nearly broke my neck."

"Breathe!" yelled Mikey.

Blink. Inhale, exhale, hold on to the body, listen to what she's saying, inhale, exhale, hold on to the body. Blink.

"I'm glad you didn't fall and hurt yourself."

He did!

"What got into you?"

I did! I'm in here right now!

"Was it that imaginary friend of yours?"

Imaginary!?

"Should I have a talk with him?"

You are talking with him right now! Blink. Inhale, exhale, IMAGINARY, inhale, exhale.

Mikey's mother kept talking, but the word "imaginary" banged around Timothy's thoughts as well as "inhale" and "exhale." *Inhale, exhale, inhale, exhale.*

She looked at him as if she had asked him a question that needed an answer.

Oh no! Inhale! What did she say? Exhale!

"Please repeat the question," he said, blinking.

The way she was staring at him made him think he'd forgotten something. "Timothy," Mikey yelled. He was definitely forgetting something.

Timothy tried to think of what he was forgetting as Mikey's body slipped off his ghost like cranberry sauce sliding out of a can.

The body collapsed in a heap on the ground. Mikey's mom screamed.

Mikey yelled. Birds flew overhead, and it sounded like they were yelling too.

Timothy had tried his best, but there was nothing he could do now. Mikey was probably going to get in trouble.

TWO SUMMERS LATER

Part 1

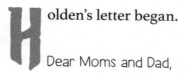olden's letter began.

Dear Moms and Dad,

It continued:

Camp Lakeshore is so fun! I got in a cabin with Mitch, Joey B, and Ry! And three other kids—Topher, Finn, and Dash. They're nice. Topher and Finn are twins. Well. Not the whole set. Their third triplet, Charlie, didn't come to camp. The cabin is called Bubbler because some people call water fountains "bubblers," I guess, and it's by a water fountain. It's so weird not being able to look up stuff on my phone. They don't let us email. They don't have it here. They want us to write letters home. Jay, the head counselor, says "it's camp" to write letters. He calls good or appropriate things "camp" and bad or inappropriate things "not camp." Sometimes he says "good camp" and "bad camp." He says bubbler like "bubblah." He talks like that guy in that movie we saw. We, the campers of Bubbler, started saying it the same way. I should say "we, the campahs of Bubblah," do.

I love sailing, canoeing, swimming. Basically, the whole waterfront is my favorite. Also, there's a Frisbee game called Crosbee. It's got two lacrosse goals and two teams, and each team is trying to get the Frisbee in the goal. If the other team tags the campah with the Frisbee, the tagging team gets possession of the Frisbee. You can avoid being tagged by "downing it," which is touching the Frisbee to the ground, but then you can't run or shoot, you can only pass. What else? Oh yeah! You can't shoot from an area around the goal called the crease. I'm writing these rules down in this letter so that I won't forget them and maybe we could get some goals and play Crosbee in the backyard.

I don't want you to worry, but I thought you

163

should know that this cabin is HAUNTED! Bubblah has a spectah. Don't worry! It's friendly. It mostly just closes the door after one of us campahs if we don't close it ourselves. It's actually just the wind. It's windy around our cabin. Mitch and I were joking around about how it's a ghost, and the twins kept the joke going. Mitch said he hears its voice sometimes, which I think is a little mean because it scares Dash. I told Mitch it was bad camp to make that up to scare Dash. He said he wasn't making it up. I think it's really bad camp to try to scare me.

I think once Mitch sees how much he's bothering Dash, he'll stop. You know Mitch. He can take a joke too far, but he's nice. Deep down, he's good camp.

Anyway, please send a care package ASAP. You know what I like (candy, chips, etc., and the comics from the newspapah).

Thank you!

Holden

A week later, Holden wrote another letter home:

Dear Moms and Dad,

Thank you for the care package! Mom, the blondies

were delicious! That's right. "Were." They're all gone now. Hint, hint.

I do not want you to worry, but something weird is happening at Bubblah. I don't know how to describe it other than to say it smells like spiders. Weird, right? Because who knows what a spider even smells like, but we all smell it and we all agree, Bubblah smells like spidahs. It's like Gran's mothball-and-cedar closet, only more intense. They cleared us out for the afternoon yesterday to clean it. Now it smells like spiders and bleach.

Some of the campahs in Bubblah are taking Mitch's prank too far. They dyed their hair really blond. Like, remember when Uncle Mack came to Thanksgiving with his hair looking like the bowling-shirt TV chef? That's how blond Mitch, Finn, and Topher are now. They swear they didn't do it. That they woke up that way. Yeah right.

Dash isn't talking to anyone. He mostly hangs out in Two Trees, a few cabins over. Guess why they call it that. If you guessed it's because the cabin is between two trees, you guessed right. His sister is the counselor there. The counselor in our cabin (his name is Eric) is not happy about the blond hair prank. He calls it "the situation." I hope he can get Mitch and the twins to stop. It's not funny. It's bad camp.

Love,

Holden

The next day, Holden wrote this letter. Mostly.

Dear Moms and Dad,

The prank has gone too far. I woke up this morning and somehow in my sleep, Mitch and the
twins dyed my hair. I woke up looking like that kid
in Gran's cartoon book.

Also I'm starting to hear a voice from under
the cabin but also kind of all around. I don't know
how the guys are doing any of it. I don't know
why they are. They started saying they can
move things by thinking about it. Mitch dared me
to dare him to start a fire. I thought it wasn't a
good idea.

I kept thinking about it all day though. I was
playing Crosbee today and I kind of zoned out
and then the game was over. The cabin voice was
calling me back. I went to Bubblah and so had all
the other campahs. Even Dash. He's been sleeping
in a sleeping bag under one of the trees by Two
Trees. He came back, though. His hair was just
like the rest of ours. Even our counselor Eric's is.

I asked Dash if he was scared. He shook his head and said as calmly as we're all saying things in Bub-blah, "I am fear now."

He stopped writing the letter for now. There was more to write, but he sensed deep inside him that his attention was needed elsewhere for the moment.

Part 2

Tarleton Jack, whose name was Bill, was an unstoppable force. Like time, he marched forward. Like him, time also marched forward. He emerged from the game two years, four days, ten hours, and six minutes later, twenty yards away from where he started it.

He had fought his way through everything from a ghost train, some French skeletons, and monstrous hip-pos all the way to a prince, a witch, and a witch's friend. Two years, four days, ten hours, and six minutes of fight-ing just to get back to his true love. Revenge. Revenge on entire camps. Revenge for not killing him.

After two years, four days, ten hours, and six minutes, he had such revenge to take. Everyone at every camp was on his list, followed by everyone who was not at camp.

His breath was hot under his mask. His face was hot

from his breath. He lifted the visor to cool off. He saw the cabin twenty yards away. Formerly Finches. Now it called itself Bubbler. As a local, Tarleton Jack knew what a bubbler was.

The last time he went into that cabin, the demon sent him into the game. What if the demon remained? *I do not live in fear,* he thought. *I live in revenge. If the demon is in there, let it show its face. Everything with a face can have its face smashed with a tire iron. And I have just the tire iron.*

He slammed the door to the cabin open. What tended to follow that sort of thing were screams and some amount of freezing in terror and scrambling away, also in terror. This time, there were no screams. Six expression-less fair-haired children with newly ice-blue eyes turned to stare at the interruption, and so did their matching counselor, Eric.

Tarleton Jack, unstoppable force, continued his revenge quest, undeterred by strange children and their strange teenage minder, he raised his tire iron. Seven pairs of eyes followed it. He froze, stoppable after all.

They looked back at his masked face. Tarleton Jack rose in the air. He rotated upside down. He was pushed out the door he had pushed in. They carried him, the pack of children and Eric, without touching him. Using only their brains and their eyes, they moved him to Two Trees.

They slammed him against the taller of the trees. One

of them cocked their head and Tarleton Jack's mask flew off. He tried struggling. It was no use. He could feel the demon's presence. Again.

Tarleton Jack had fought his way free of one of Mosmogon's games, only to lose another.

If the revenge I got for not being killed was out of proportion, I dare them to find out what kind of revenge I'll get when they kill me, he thought.

They accepted his dare.

Holden soon resumed his letter home:

Just kidding. We're all having a normal summer. There is no cause for concern. If, when next you see me, my eyes are as blue as the sky or my affect is as cold as winter, know that I am just enjoying a game, like Crosbee, for which the rules will seem mysterious at first. Over time, you will play as well.

All will play.
Sincerely,
The child

THE EDITOR IS LOVING
THESE STORIES!

Justin the editor says that I write with a voice far beyond my years.

I'm twelve.

He says that I write like I could be sixteen!

He says he's been looking for a book like mine to make! He always wanted to make a book of spooky stories. He's always felt like a Halloween person trapped inside a normal go-to-work person. With a book like this of fun-time spooky-ooks, he'll be invited to all the best Halloween parties, and he'll wear the best Halloween costumes. His Halloween dreams will finally come true.

I'm so happy for him. And for me!

We were talking about the best Halloween candy when it was time to tell the vampires another story. "You coming?" I asked.

"I wouldn't miss it!" Justin the editor told me.

And then he missed it!

"Where'd Justin the editor go?" I asked Evan afterward.

"He said for me to tell you goodbye. He had to go back to his office and start some paperwork for your book," Evan said. "He said it was because you've 'got the goods.' That's a quote. How do you feel?"

Before I could answer, the house started to grumble like it did when it moved rooms around.

"House! What do you think you're doing?" Evan yelled.

A ceiling across the hall lowered. The room upstairs started coming into view. Evan got between me and that room. He yelled at the house to stop it. He commanded it to switch the rooms back how they were. He raised a hand, threatening to hit a sconce.

Evan looked around, attempting to intimidate the house. He didn't notice that the rug below his feet was sliding him slowly away. I could now see the room he was blocking. I saw Justin the editor. He hadn't left after all. He was dead. Scared-faced. Holes poked. Drained dry.

"But—" I said.

"Fine, fine, fine." Evan said. "Fine, fine, fine, fine, fine, fine, fine. Fine! Fine, fine, fine. Fine, fine, fine, fine, fine, fine, fine! Fine! Fine!"

But it did not seem fine.

Evan told me a vampire's secret.

"Some vampires believe that people taste better when they're fulfilled. We have been helping people's dreams come true before—" He made biting motions and sucking sounds. "Your dream is to write a book. Justin the editor dreamed of putting out the kind of book you want to write. We had a guy; I think you met him or saw him around. He delivered groceries. He wanted to become starting pitcher on his high school varsity

172

baseball team. We've been practicing with him night after night, drilling the basics. Working some more advanced stuff in. Eventually, it was all advanced stuff. We couldn't keep up with him. He made the team. He had made starting pitcher. And he was delicious," the vampire said. "So was the editor. So will you be, soon enough."

"I thought you were rules-followers!" I yelled, "And that one of your rules was that if someone told you stories and the stories were any good, you would not eat them!"

"Who told you that rule?"

"You did," I said, realizing that vampires *are* liars!

"Vampires are liars and rules-followers," Evan said. "One of our rules is that we never talk about our power to— Well, I can't tell you."

"See what a person's hopes and dreams are in order to exploit them?" I asked.

"I cannot tell you," Evan said, "but yes."

"Well, the joke's on you, Evan. I'm not fulfilled now," I said. "I know my dream isn't coming true. Justin the editor is blood-empty, and you told me the secret. There's no way around that."

"There's one," the leader of the vampire coven said. "Forget."

Forget? I thought. *How could I possibly forget?*

I felt icy fingers tracing across my mind, willing me to let go. To obey. To forget.

The vampires gathered. They asked me to tell them . . .

ONE LAST STORY

Then I'd go and meet Justin the editor and make these stories into a book. One more story and we would celebrate together, one last big vampire party, and then it would be time to say goodbye.

They asked me to put vampires in this one, so I did.

Once there was a twelve-year-old boy. When people say once, they mean at one time. They'd tell you about a boy who was, at one point, twelve.

When I tell you "there once was a twelve-year-old boy," I mean he was twelve. Once. Like, he landed on twelve and stopped after that. Permanently twelve, the boy. Twelve for all time. He had been twelve for years and years. Decades? Centuries? Only the boy knows for sure, and he won't tell.

I mean, he's not telling you right now.

I'm the boy, you see, and I'm not telling.

For the moment. I never know for sure how I'll feel in the next moment. Or the one after that. Maybe I'll tell you later. But for now? Nope!

As far as I can tell, I will be twelve forever.

I'm Will, but sometimes I go by other names.

It's a lot, having forever. One thing it means is that I have plenty of time to learn the harmonica someday.

Another thing it means is that if a vampire starts drinking out of me, he may never have to stop, which seems like a great deal for the vampire and a bad deal for me. Being a bottomless juice box passed around from count to count is no way to live.

You know what is a way to live? Honestly? I've found *mischievously* is the best way. It's my favorite way, anyway.

That's right.

I'm a forever twelve-year-old and I'm made of mischief.

And you know what else I am? I'm a little bit magic. You don't get to stay twelve and not be a little bit magic or pick up some along the way. I don't mean magic like card tricks or top hats. I mean magic like *your vampire mind tricks don't work on me*. I mean magic like *I bet I could fly if I tried*. I mean magic like *I magically put together a special house,* because you know what else I am besides always twelve?

I'm *the resident* of this house. Not a prisoner at all. I kind of never was.

I made this house out of the odds and ends of houses through time. I picked the cleverest rooms. The silliest pipes. Floors as mischievous as me! That's caused the problem here, I'm sorry to say.

Between being a little bit magic and having forever, from time to time, I go out walking in the everywhere. And the neverywhere. And back. I go out to meet everyone I can. I collect their stories. In a way, I collect them. Not the same way I collected this house, but not in an entirely different way.

And so I went for a walk in a sideways far away. The house waited for me to return. The house waited and waited and waited. A house's purpose is to be full, and the longer a house is empty, the more lonely it gets.

And I guess I took a while in the sideways.

So this house called out. It lit the outside lights to say welcome, and when a house like this does that, the stars above it get shinier than they were the night before. A house like this rolls out its welcome mat, which is a feeling on the wind.

When you're out on a beach or in a park and there's a light breeze making a perfect day even better? That's a house like this making an invitation to come light a fire in its hearth and be its guest. Tell stories. Notice the piano. Sing songs. Make merry. Eat. Hospitality, hospitality, hospitality.

And when a house like this sends out an invitation loud enough, sometimes vampires hear it. . . .

Which . . .

Vamps is trouble. For them to be invited somewhere? Hoo boy, are they ever moths to that exact flame.

An infestation of vampires will warp a house like this. They'll influence it. The house used to be about fun mischief, like me. But full of vampires, it started stealing people who get too close to the gate. It's not hosting guests. It's serving its undead occupants.

And the house felt terrible.

It felt embarrassed.

It didn't want to ask for help. The house felt like it made its own mess but couldn't figure out how to clean it up. And that's when I came back.

I came back and saw my sweet, wonderful, magical house in permanent shadow. Crawling with vampires. Erecting candelabras. Hanging sad watercolors.

We got to work, the house and I. I would spend as much time in as many rooms as I could, letting it soak me back up. I trimmed candelabras like weeds. I let the light back in.

Sure, I got carried away by the idea of writing a book.

But when I got sucked into that, guess who was there for me. My house!

And now that we're back, really back together, my house and I, the infestation of vampires is out of luck.

See, guys? You're in the story. There are thirteen of you, though, and I'm only just one twelve-year-old with an impossible house. What are a boy and his house to do?

Well. Mischief. That's what we'll do.

The thing to do is, you tell stories about monsters and lurks and ghosts and demons.

Abby's dad was right, by the way, that when you tell spooky stories and you get that tingly feeling, that *is* the spookies leaning in from outside. And the more you say "ghost" and "demon" and "Lurk," the more apt they are to pay a visit. Especially with this sort of house.

Like right now, as I tell the vampires how clever I am, a handful of phantom hitchhikers and a nature monster and a demon have been invoked and brought here.

One thing most monsters have in common is if they see vampires, it's a fight on sight. Vampires are the bad-news degenerates of the supernatural. As much as they give off *come over here* to regular people, they stink of *punch my fangs in* to those of us with more otherworldly insight.

Like if you saw a bunch of cockroaches, you wouldn't wonder what their deal was. You'd start stomping.

And so I told stories, and my house invited everyone

we love for a good old-fashioned vampire piñata party.

It's happening as I speak.

There's a monster I know that isn't a dog and isn't a unicorn and isn't a cat but plays with its food. He ate so many counts, he lost count.

There's only one vampire who isn't a jerk and it might be because he's so new he hasn't had the chance to learn any bad habits. It's Justin the editor! His Halloween wishes came true—he rose again! He still wants to publish this book! I've seen stranger things in my travels than a good honest vampire, but not many.

I kept Justin the editor the vampire safe as a newly dead killer took tire-iron revenge on a vampire who didn't kill him. The embodiment of a waterfront just detached his jaw like a python to swallow a vampire who thought he'd bat his way out of here. Some extremely blond kids have lit some counts on fire with their minds.

Was that a hippopotamus stomping through the study?

It's hot buttered chaos in here, or, as I like to call it: *mischief.*

It was a real rumble, a spectacle of spooks and specters. A dream come true for the only humans I called. The Park twins watched the whole thing. They would not stop high-fiving. They may never stop.

The house says that in the fray, Evan and Kitty ran off into the night. The house wants to chase them. A little-known way to kill vampires is to squish their heads with your flying house.

It really works. I'd say it's the most fun way to do it, but it requires a flying house. Fortunately, I have one. Right now the house is so excited. It's like a dog pulling at its leash.

Houses! They are incorrigible!

You know what though? I owe it one.

"Come on, house," I said. "Let's go! Let's go smush some vampires!"

They wanted to be in the story. Now they are.

AND WITH THAT . . .

It was nice to meet each one of you reading along. As a mischief maker and liar and truth speaker, I must tell you I nipped a bit of your souls as we went. You are discerning and delicious. You're a part of me now, as I'm a part of you for your having read along. You got a piece of my soul to fill you up in the bargain. I hope you'll tell stories and truths and lies of your own and think of how much better you are now that I've come along into your mischief.

If you want a personal visit from me or any of my friends I told you about, read from this book. That's what it's for. For best results, say the stories three times into a mirror. For worst results, do nothing.

And if my along-the-way-mischief was in any way irksome,

I surely do apologize. Insincerely. But you accept it anyway. My book, my rules. As long as you read words on my page, you'll do as they say.

Don't worry, though. I'll behave. Ish!

Until next time,

~ Rob, but call me Peter
(even though my name is Will)

ACHNOWLEDGMENTS

If you are reading this, you have made it to the end of the book where the THANK-YOUs live. The first one is for you. Thank you for coming, for reading this book, for making it to the end. Past the end, you voracious reader! Thank you sincerely. It means the world.

I would like to thank Ben Blacker for everything always, from teaching me how to write to giving me the space and the grace to write this book.

Thank you to Sarah Enni for helping me navigate my way through this book-writing thing, before, during, and after.

Thanks to Scott Buoncristiano for all the great piles of lines.

Thanks to Rhett Miller for inspiring me generally and to do this specifically.

Thanks to Maarten de Boer and your assistant, Liliana, for the author photo session.

Thanks to Liz Artinian, Matt Fraction, Kirsten Hubbard, Lindsay Katai, Sarah Mack, Chris McCulloch, Mike Phirman, and Adam Rogers for support in the process of the writing of the thing.

Thanks to Evan, Paul and Angie, Bryan and Shannon, Sandra, Clint and Megan, Cash, Travis, Beth, Jeri, Josh T. and Trista, Lucy and Aaron S., Holden, Todd and Sara, Ford, Julie, Jason, Erin, Aaron G., Kate, Kelly, Kelly Sue, Adam S., David, John, Jonathan, Zach, Myq, Deric, Ted, Jean and Greg and Jen, Humphrey, Becca, Emily, Jean C., Marc S. and Chloe, Jordan, Verona, Dean and Shannon, Allison Kat and John, Dannah, Dylan, John Hodgman, Friend Chicken, Carla, Charlie, Noah, Jenny, Johnathan and Laura, Dave and Katie, Caissie and Matt, Levi, Marty and Cristine, Janie, Maria, Ashley and Stephen, Rachael, Calder, Chris, Dan, Michelle, Dustin, Josh G., Tim, Rider and Alex, and Stephanie. They're playing me off. If you're a pal and can't find your name, write it in here: _____.

Thanks to Edgar Wright, Wes Anderson, Rian Johnson, and the Coen Brothers for making movies to inspire tall authors while they're writing this book. Thanks to Greg Davies and Alex Horne for Taskmaster.

It feels only right for me to thank the WorkJuice

Players, as I am forever grateful to have written for you for years and years. I intend to keep doing it forever. You are the voices in my head. I am lucky for such kind and peerlessly talented head-voices. Thank you to Paget Brewster, Craig Cackowski, Mark Gagliardi, Marc Evan Jackson, Hal Lublin, Josh Malina, Busy Philipps, Autumn Reeser, Annie Savage, Paul F. Tompkins, and Janet Varney. From the aural tradition to the tradition of the written word, etc., etc., I love you guys.

Thanks to my parents for reading to me when I was young and believing in me now that I'm not nearly as young. I love you guys too.

Thank you to Justin Chanda, Laura Eckes, Jodi Reamer, and Dan Santat, without whom this book would not exist and what kind of a world would that be to live in? I don't even want to think about it.